10-06

Further praise for Helen Humphreys

Wild Dogs

"Humphreys maintains the same spare, unflinching honesty throughout, whether writing from the perspective of a brilliantly stoic scientist or a brain-damaged young girl. . . . Its brutal perspective on love and loss will haunt you for days."
— *Entertainment Weekly*

"Told from various points of view, this evocative, unpredictable, and frightening story poetically parses the meaning of wildness. . . . Versatile and nervy Canadian novelist Humphreys . . . delves into the deepest mysteries of existence with empathy, imagination, and an earthy and thrilling lyricism."
— *Booklist*, starred review

"Humphreys poignantly captures the uneasy camaraderie that can arise among strangers."
— *Publishers Weekly*

The Lost Garden

"A stunningly beautiful little gem that lingers in the memory like the heady scent of a damask rose."
— Karen Campbell, *Boston Globe*

"A beautiful evocation of love and loss. . . . Subtle and deeply affecting. . . . Rich and satisfying."
— Carmela Ciuraru, *Minneapolis Star-Tribune*

"[A] finely wrought novel. . . . Humphreys's writing is equally capable of sparkling dialogue and lyrical description."
— Margot Livesey, *New York Times Book Review*
(selected as a *New York Times* Notable Book of 2002)

"Measured, lyrical. . . . Humphreys is a metaphysical novelist; for her, intricate emotional content finds specific analogues in the made world— . . . an overgrown garden that, once cleared, reveals its consoling secrets."

—*The New Yorker*

"Helen Humphrey's affecting novel never fails to couple the realistic with the ideal, the historical with the timeless. . . . A refreshingly unabashed attempt to locate the indelible but so often secreted nature of love and loss."

—Matthew Batt, *San Francisco Chronicle*

"This novel reconstructs a held-breath moment in time and the emotional education of a woman who has never felt loved. It remains with the reader long after the last page is turned, and it feels like an evening walk through a pungent, private garden."

—Beth Kephart, *Book*

WILD DOGS

a novel

HELEN HUMPHREYS

W. W. Norton & Company NEW YORK LONDON

For information about permission to reproduce selections from
this book, write to Permissions, W. W. Norton & Company, Inc.,
500 Fifth Avenue, New York, NY 10110

Manufacturing by Courier Westford
Production manager: Anna Oler

Library of Congress Cataloging-in-Publication Data

Humphreys, Helen, 1961–
Wild dogs : a novel / Helen Humphreys. —1st American ed.
p. cm.
ISBN 0-393-06015-2 (hardcover)
1. Human-animal relationships—Fiction. 2. Wilderness
areas—Fiction. 3. Women dog owners—Fiction. 4. Animal
welfare—fiction. 5. Zoologists—Fiction. 6. Feral dogs—Fiction.
I. Title.
PR9199.3.H822W55 2005
813'.54—dc22   2005000262

ISBN-13: 978-0-393-32842-4 pbk.
ISBN-10: 0-393-32842-2 pbk.

W. W. Norton & Company, Inc.
500 Fifth Avenue, New York, N.Y. 10110
www.wwnorton.com

W. W. Norton & Company Ltd.
Castle House, 75/76 Wells Street, London W1T 3QT

1 2 3 4 5 6 7 8 9 0

As I lay dying
  the woman with the dog's eyes
  would not close my eyes for me . . .

—Homer, *The Odyssey*, Book XI
translated by William Faulkner

one

alice

The wild dogs roam the summer fields just outside of town. Their eyes flash, bright stars in the woods at night, and they weave like fire through the dry grass towards the edge of the city, looking for something to kill and eat.

Love is like those wild dogs. If it hunts you down, it will not let you go. And what you can never know from the beginning is how hard or how long you'll love something; how even when it has gone the love you felt will still chase you down, loping like dark flame through your blood.

The wild dogs are real. They are out there, beyond the safety of the streets and houses, beyond the lights of the city. And one of those wild dogs is mine.

There are six of us who gather most evenings at the woods behind the fields on Cooper's farm. We arrive at twilight and stay well after dark. Sometimes we stand together and sometimes we are strung out along the treeline, calling into the woods, our voices lifting as prayer to the soft ear of darkness.

We are calling our dogs back. There are nights when we cry out and nothing happens, and then there are nights when the woods crackle with running weight and the pack of wild dogs bursts out in front of us and we surge forward, uttering the human names that used to belong to them.

It is the strangest feeling to see my dog running towards me with no glimmer of recognition in her eyes. How can I still know her and she not know me at all? She runs out from the trees, before me and then past me, running across the fields of Cooper's farm, and it is as though I have lost not only her, but myself.

Sometimes the dogs are so close that we can smell them. They smell warm and acrid, not unpleasant, but not familiar. They run so near that I can see how their fur has become matted and knotted with burrs. I can see who limps and who is getting thinner.

But they don't return to us. We come out to the woods every evening and call to the dogs, and they never come back. And it is not about love, although we love the dogs fiercely. But the dogs didn't understand our love when they lived with us and certainly they don't understand it now. Whatever they felt for us then wasn't what we know of love. No, it is not about love. It is about belonging. Once we belonged with those dogs, belonged to them, and now that they've left us we don't know who we are.

Wild is a word I would have once given to my younger self; that child who ran fast through the woods or swam the river swollen with flood water. I can still feel the flex of that river, feel how fast and far it moved me along its length so that when I clambered up the muddy bank on the other side I was a good half mile from where I'd started. The river had taken me and yet I had not relented once against its force. That was how I lived then. That was what I thought wild was—throwing myself totally into something, at something, letting it move me, but never quite surrendering to it.

I grew into a more reckless person; had sex young, drank and took drugs, rode a motorcycle. I would have said all that was being wild.

The motorcycle was the best part of that, really. I rode it for years, ten years in fact, selling my latest bike only when I got the dog and realized the two things were incompatible.

After I left school I worked at a car wash in the centre of this small city where I live. I used to ride the motorcycle to work, as I rode it everywhere. I would get on the highway at a quarter to five in the morning, slip through the loosened knot of darkness into daylight. The road twisted beside the river all the way down into the city; twisted like the river. The dull orange highway lights went out, one by one, above me. There's a heightened feeling to riding a bike because it's such a vulnerable act. Any small mistake can kill you, and so one must feel very alive to compensate, to balance out the danger and fear. I can recall that feeling easily. And I can remember the smells of the early morning—the tang of the river beside the road, the hot steel of the cars that swept by me.

I rode that motorcycle in all weather, through every daylight hour, onto the shoulder of winter. I rode with rain nailing the visor of my helmet shut and with lightning pinning the ground on either side of me. I rode with raingear on, dry and sweating inside an envelope of yellow plastic; and I rode through unexpected storms in my jeans and jacket, water pooling at my crotch and the dye from my gloves staining my hands black for weeks.

To ride in cold is to feel the body slowly stiffen at all its hinges. It is to ride tucked down behind the small windshield, with the left hand cupped above the heat rising from the engine cylinders. To ride in hot weather is to smell the bitter diesel of the tarmac, to feel the pock of bees exploding on your jacket and visor.

What I remember best—the feel of the wind against my shoulders, how the resistance felt exactly like two hands pushing at me. When I was tired I could lean into that wind and it would hold me upright in the saddle. How it felt to ride out in early morning and disturb the mist in the hollows; how much cooler it was to ride through the dip at the bottom of a hill; how it smelled like rain and felt damp and gentle on my skin; how the early morning landscape was like an X-ray of all the secret places where water had touched down. There were pools of gauzy white in the dark, grey dawn. I felt them all on my skin, and this is what I thought it meant to be alive.

Wild, I could say that about myself then, and yet now I can see that it wasn't really true. To be wild is to live by instinct and not by imagination. To live wild is to have no story for it.

I would have still said I was wild, that night we went to the bar to talk about the dogs. Then I could still recognize the feeling I thought of as wild. I would have called it back using that name.

We sat downstairs by the open window. It was almost September and stormy outside. The rain showed the boughs on the trees as black and the wind stirred the leaves into a kind of restless fury. I sat opposite you, our heads almost touching across the small table. We drank and talked about the dogs. I don't remember what we said, but I knew I was worried about my dog, Hawk, and how she'd survive the winter living in those woods. The weather was already turning. Summer was stiffening along September's edge, hardening into the ambiguity of autumn.

The bar was mostly empty. It was a weeknight, around suppertime, and most people were happily elsewhere. When I went upstairs to use the bathroom, the entire upper floor was dark and empty. I started walking across the room, from the staircase to the washrooms at the back, and my feet kicked through something covering the carpet. Leaves. The entire floor was blanketed in leaves. They must have blown in from the open window downstairs where we were sitting. They must have blown in and swirled up the staircase, fluttered to the carpet as though to the soft forest floor. I had not seen any of this happening. And it was then I knew that I must love you.

And when I came back out of the bathroom, there you

were, standing in the middle of the floor in the ankle-deep leaves. We didn't say anything. I walked over to you and took your hands and leaned in to kiss you. I could smell the sharp damp of the leaves and I could feel my heart riding up against my ribs, that vocabulary of nerves and feeling that it sometimes remembers how to find.

How do we know anyone or anything? Did I know Hawk because I knew her habits?

I had my dog for four years, from the time she was a seven-week-old puppy, and in all that time she slept sprawled out on the end of my bed. She was a big adult dog, shepherd/collie mix, and I often had to sleep with my legs curled up to accommodate her bulk. I never minded doing this, although some of the people who shared my bed over those four years took issue with the dog's being there. It was not negotiable, I always said. Hawk was here first. She was allowed to stay.

And then, several months before I lost her, Hawk changed her sleeping patterns, deciding to remain downstairs on the couch instead of coming up to sleep with me. I have no idea what prompted this; there seemed to be no reason for this change in behaviour. It was as if she'd grown weary of her habits and had felt the need to make something new of her life. Whatever the reason, I accepted the changes in the dog without protest, something I would never have done with a person. But I trusted that the dog knew what was right for herself better than I could. I trusted that the gulf between our natures resulted in her being the wiser creature, and I knew that her decision to alter her sleeping arrangements had nothing to do with me. I didn't need to take it personally.

There were other changes Hawk had made in her life, other breaks in the recognizable pattern. She used to enjoy swimming and then, one day, she wouldn't go near the water. She used to ride in the front seat of the car and then changed to sitting in the back, as though she was being chauffeured. These are seemingly unimportant things, really, but they can't be explained by my human logic and so they continue to perplex me. If there's no apparent reason for something to change, then why does it? Is it a dog's nature to vary behaviour when life becomes too comfortable? Is it ours? Because that's what really scares me, that the stability and security I constantly tell myself I'm seeking—were they ever achieved—would be disrupted and destroyed by that same part of me that exists in Hawk, that same part that made her move from her comfortable perch on the end of my bed to the hard, lumpy downstairs couch. It scares me to think that I could give up, easily, all that I desire.

I love the dog. But there's no need to mention that, not really. She has been my stability and security through these last four years. I could say that instead. And what I can't believe is that she's gone from me. I can't believe I won't see her big furry head at the living-room window when I come home from work, or feel her lean against my leg when I stand at the sink in the evening, washing dishes. I can't believe my life is now only moments without her.

It was John who sent Hawk away. He'd lost his job months ago and we'd been fighting ever since. He had never liked the dog, I can see that now, how he was jealous of the place Hawk occupied in my affections. Other people in town, other people he knew who had lost their jobs at the factory, had got rid of their dogs because they could no longer afford to feed them. That is what he did with my dog. That was his excuse. It took me three days to get him to divulge where he'd taken her, and by the time I drove out to the fields back of Cooper's farm, my dog was part of the pack that lived in the woods there and she wouldn't come back to me.

There has been a pack of wild dogs living in the woods behind Cooper's farm for a while now. Whether the dogs wandered there themselves or were dumped at the edge of the woods, no one knows. Now, though, I have learnt that if someone wants to get rid of a dog, they drive it out to the woods and leave it there.

"It's not the same as killing her," John had said. "I could have done that—others have done that—but I didn't. She just lives somewhere else now. Not with us."

There are six of us who wait every evening at the edge of the woods. There is Malcolm, a man in his forties who lives with his mother in an old farmhouse not far from Cooper's farm. "I live there because she had a stroke," he said defensively, the first time we found out about his situation. "She needed someone to look after her. I had to move back." Malcolm's dog is an apricot standard poodle named Sidney. He got away by accident. Malcolm had been out of town for two days and the neighbour in charge of walking the dog had let him out unattended, instead of putting him on a leash and taking him out along the road.

There is Lily, a tiny girl in her twenties, and I say *girl* because she's got something wrong with her, some level of retardation that keeps her young and guileless as a child. She has called her dog simply "Dog," and when we ask her the breed, she says again, "Dog." Her parents set Dog free out here because they said Lily wasn't looking after her.

"But I was," she says, whenever she tells the story. "I looked after that dog just fine."

Jamie is thirteen, a scruffy kid with ripped jeans and a dirty T-shirt. His dog's name is Scout. "Pit bull," he says before I ask him. "Stepfather." For this is how we tell our stories. Our name. The name of the dog. The breed. Who sent the dog away. Jamie rides his bike out to the woods every evening, drops it hard on the grass, and walks quickly up and down in front of the trees, calling his dog's name so sharp and fast it sounds like gunfire.

Walter Pendleton's dog is a Jack Russell terrier named Georgie. It seems odd that so small a dog would fit into a pack of considerably larger dogs. But Walter has seen Georgie running near the middle of the pack. "Nowhere near last," he says proudly. He is old, Walter Pendleton, and I guess Georgie is too, which makes it all the more miraculous that he has been accepted into the pack of wild dogs. This fact has cheered us into thinking that what lives in the woods and runs across the fields at night is perhaps still closer to being dog than wolf. But it doesn't explain why the dogs won't come back to us, even though we stand by the woods calling for them every night.

There are two other people who meet every evening at the edge of the trees. There is me, and there is you.

Your dog is wolf already. You got him last summer when you were living far north of here observing a wolf pack. He was a pup then and his mother had been shot.

"I shouldn't have taken him," you say. "I should have just let him die." As a wildlife biologist, as a scientist, you're not supposed to get emotionally involved with your research.

You called the wolf pup "Lopez," and you brought him with you when you came to town this August to use the university library and write up your notes. Lopez had to be walked on a rope because he was unpredictable around people and other dogs. But you always felt sorry for him, being tethered, and so one day you brought him out here, behind the fields on Cooper's farm, and you let him run free. And this is exactly what he did. He ran into the woods and joined the pack of wild dogs.

I don't know what happiness means. I think about it a lot because that is the name I have given to the short time I had with you, but I'm not sure it's the proper thing to call those moments. But what else can I say about them? The language that I have now is not adequate to the feelings that I had then.

I remember one day in particular. I had come back to the cabin early, and as I drove down the long driveway, you were walking ahead of me. You were carrying scissors (I never asked why), and at first you didn't hear the sound of the car. You were walking easily down the driveway, flanked by tall meadow grasses, your back straight and your long arms bent at the elbows—you hardly ever had them fully extended in anything you did—and I tried to make you turn towards me with the sheer force of my feeling for you. But it didn't work. I stopped the car and sounded the horn and then you looked back, turned around, and walked towards me.

It is impossible to fully inhabit a moment again. That is part of the inherent sorrow of life. This can never be that. I can never really let you know how much I felt for you that August afternoon. I can just choose one small point to describe and hope that I can describe it well enough to make it real again.

So I choose this. You are almost at the car. I roll down the window, and in the space before you lean in and kiss me, the space before I look into your eyes and think, for the thousandth time, how yours is the right face, the perfect face; in that brief interval before we renew our connection, the scent of the hot summer afternoon tumbles through the car window. What is the smell? Dry, dusty heat and the straw-like musk of the field grasses. And overlaying everything, the scent of milkweed. It's a scent like lilac, but deeper. A descent. Footfalls at dusk. The rise of memory. It's what a bruise would smell like, or the inside of a promise. It's shyness at the point when feeling enters conversation and the words stumble over one another.

All I have now is this backwards glance. I've lost your face framed by the car window, the exact look in your eyes, the things we said, how your skin felt under my fingertips. I've lost all that, but I can still hold onto that one moment when I rolled the window down and the summer spilled into the car and it smelled of us.

I was working that summer pumping gas. It was a job I had done years before and there was a certain indignity in having to return to it now. But work was hard to find and I was lucky to have landed anything at all. And really, I minded pumping gas less than a lot of other things I've done for money. At least I got to be alone in the cash booth and I could read when business was slow. Sunny days I generally had a pretty good time of it. But there were always twice as many cars to service on a rainy day.

We were living on my pathetic wages from pumping gas. John had been let go when the furniture factory closed, and because he wouldn't demean himself by doing something as base as pumping gas, he hadn't been able to find any other work. Instead of being grateful that I was bringing money in for us to live on, John resented my working and constantly picked fights with me about the smallest, most insignificant things. I hadn't given him a phone message. I made too much noise in the mornings getting ready for work. He was critical of everything I did, everything I said, and it was easy to leave him after he sent my dog away. We had been together for only a couple of years and even in the first year, when he was employed and relatively happy, there were plenty of moments when I questioned my decision to be with him. So it was easy to leave him, as I've said, and even without the fact of his getting rid of Hawk, the leaving felt inevitable. Leaving John was not a mistake. What was a mistake was what I decided to do after I left him.

The six of us who gathered at the edge of the woods out back of Cooper's farm connected with one another swiftly and strongly. Because we had suffered the same loss we bonded with an immediacy that I now realize was premature and foolish. If I were to do anything over, I would not have gone to live in the cabin on Malcolm's property. And perhaps I would not have fallen in love with you.

I left John in a hurry, in a fit of rage, after I found out what he'd done and after I realized Hawk wasn't coming back. I threw some clothes and books into my car and slept for the next two nights in the parking lot of the gas station where I worked. The third evening I was standing with the others at the edge of the woods and you asked me why I looked so tired.

"I've been sleeping in my car," I said. "I left my boyfriend."

Malcolm, who was standing on the other side of me, was quiet for a moment and then he said, "There's a small cabin on my property that's not being used right now. You could have it for the rest of the summer if you wanted."

I followed Malcolm home that evening. He lived on one of the county roads, not far from Cooper's farm. The driveway was dirt, rutted, and sprouting a band of waist-high grass down the centre. The grass made a pinging, percussive noise on the underside of the car as I drove over it.

We went past the farmhouse, a dilapidated white-frame

building, and Malcolm stopped his car on the other side of a collapsing barn. Out front of the barn were rusted cars, an old freezer, and the remains of two iron bedsteads.

A little way behind the barn, on the bank of a small stream, was an old log cabin. There was moss growing on the roof and the screen door was hanging off by one hinge.

"It hasn't been lived in for a while," said Malcolm apologetically. "It was the original building on this property once. It's almost two hundred years old."

We stepped up onto the rotting front porch and he opened the cabin door. The interior was dark and smelled of mice. There was a fireplace on the wall across from the door, a bed under the left window, and a table under the right. The floor of the cabin was dusty and covered with bits of wood and what looked like chewed-up pieces of toilet paper.

"You can use the stream for washing," said Malcolm, "but you'll have to bring water in for drinking. I can lend you a camp stove. There's one in the barn somewhere."

He jammed his hands into the front pockets of his khakis and rocked back and forth on the balls of his feet. He was a nervous sort of man, Malcolm, and I could never decide what he was being nervous about.

This is what I knew about Malcolm Dodd. He lived with his mother in the farmhouse where he'd been raised. He sold antiques, and this required him to travel out of town for several days every month. He had a dog named Sidney who now lived in the forest with my dog, Hawk. He was probably in his early forties, judging from the lines on his face, his receding hairline, and the soft basket of belly that hung over the waistband of his pants.

I had grown up in this town but I didn't have any real friends left here. Most people I knew had moved away after finishing school, or after the factory had closed down. My mother was dead, and I was no longer in contact with my father. I knew the people I worked with and some of the people John had worked with, who had stayed, but I didn't know anyone well enough to sleep on their couch for a while, or to ask their opinion as to whether I should move into the empty cabin on Malcolm Dodd's property. I'm sure if I'd had friends in town, they would have advised against this decision.

"Thank you," I said to Malcolm. "I really appreciate this."

He looked both pleased and embarrassed, rocking back and forth on his feet. At the time I didn't wonder why he hadn't asked me over to the farmhouse to meet his mother, but as I lay on the narrow bed that first night, under the dusty blankets, it occurred to me that perhaps Malcolm hadn't told his mother I would be living in the cabin. Perhaps I was his secret.

I lay in that cabin with you. We were naked, lying on our sides after sex, facing each other. You ran your hand lightly from my shoulder, over my ribs, hip bone, and halfway down the outside of my leg, as far as you could reach. It is how I imagined you used to stroke your wolf dog, and when I looked at your face I could see that you were watching yourself touch me.

"Do you think they are happier without us?" I asked.

"No," you said. "I don't. I don't think it's about happiness at all."

I leaned over and kissed you, and then I ran my finger over your lips and you opened your mouth. I could feel the sharp, serrated edges of your teeth, and the soft inside of your lower lip. I thought of all the times I had been so miserable and how I would walk the dog barefoot in the early mornings in the park across from where I lived—the dog without a leash, plodding behind me through the soft grass. Every so often I would fish a biscuit from my pocket and reach down to slip it inside Hawk's mouth. She would take it so gently I could feel the rubbery curl of her lip and the ridge of the roof of her mouth and this would console me— that I trusted the dog not to bite me, and that she trusted me to put my hand into her mouth.

When you and Hawk were both gone from my life, I missed you more. I knew you for such a short time, but you came into my life with the force to change it forever. Hawk was simply a part of my existing life and she was memorialized in everything I continued to do without her. Driving the car, I could almost see her thick, barrel-chested furry body sitting up straight in the seat beside me. If I braked too suddenly, she would balance her forepaws against the dashboard, and when I reversed the car she would push one of her hind legs against the seat-back in an effort to stay balanced. When I walk anywhere it is easy to imagine her trotting along beside me, stopping to sniff the air or breaking into a sprint when she spots a squirrel far enough away from a tree for her to have hope in the chase.

But there is not the luxury of habit to sustain the memory of you. We had moments, not routines. There's nothing left of you but what I can remember and what I make up, and I fear that soon they will become indistinguishable.

One of the first things the group of us did was to try to lure the dogs out of the woods with food. We left mounds of dog biscuits on the grass in front of the trees. Sure enough, when we returned the next evening, the biscuits would have disappeared. But the problem was that whoever was eating the dog biscuits wouldn't come out to eat them while we were there. It could have been our dogs, but it could just as easily have been squirrels or raccoons or field mice.

After meeting fruitlessly for days at the edge of the woods, the six of us who have lost our dogs decide to actively memorialize them. We do this by taking the others on the walks we used to take the dogs.

Lily goes first. Lily lives in a small apartment building in the centre of the city. It is a long bus ride from the edge of town to the centre, and as we bump along on the city bus I marvel at Lily's persistence and dedication in coming out to the edge of the woods every evening. She sits very upright on the bench seat, watching out the window. If any of us try to talk to her during the bus ride, she gets anxious and cuts us off after one or two remarks. She is obviously someone who can't concentrate on more than one thing at a time and right now she is concentrating on following the route home.

The bus passes farmhouses, an auto body shop, a wrecking yard with a mangy German shepherd chained to the inside of the gate. Then there's strip mall after strip mall, each one punctuated by a doughnut shop or fast-food restaurant.

Lily has dirty-blonde hair that hangs limply to her shoulders. She has nervous eyes that flicker from thing to thing, the way a mouse darts out from its hiding place and then darts back again. She holds onto the metal pole in front of her seat with both hands and she wears a cardigan that is buttoned up to the neck, even though it's August. The cardigan is partly there to hide the red stain that creeps from her jaw down her neck and probably across the skin of her chest and shoulders, the parts we can't see because they are covered by the sweater.

We know what happened to Lily because you asked her early on and then you told the rest of us. Lily had lived with her parents and her baby brother in a wooden house in another city. The parents had been out at a neighbour's one night and Lily had set the house on fire by lighting candles under a vase of dried flowers. She had only meant to make a cosy light, this is what she said to you and what you said to us. She had only wanted to make a cosy light. She spent too much time trying to extinguish the fire, and by the time she realized that it was impossible, the whole house was ablaze. She got badly burned trying to rescue her brother from the room where he slept upstairs. She did get him out, we learn later, and, when they tried to give her grafts to repair her burned skin, she went into shock on the operating table and stopped breathing. By the time they managed to get her breathing again she'd lost some brain function. Her baby brother has since left home and Lily still lives with her parents.

We troop off the bus and stand in front of the decrepit apartment building, looking up at the stack of identical balconies above us.

"It was the barking," says Lily.

"What was?" says Jamie. He has come on this venture somewhat reluctantly. "Okay, since it's on my way home anyway," he'd said. He's wary of Lily, doesn't approve of her naming her dog Dog. "Not a name," he said, which sent her into a bit of a panic. "It can't be *not* a name because it *is* a name," she pointed out rather hysterically.

"There was no barking and no dogs," says Lily. "That is why they made Dog leave."

"No dogs allowed in the building," explains Walter Pendleton.

We stare up at the rusted balconies and then you take Lily gently by the arm.

"Where did you walk her?" you ask.

Lily leads us around the side of the building to the common grassy space at the back, splattered here and there with desultory playground equipment and the occasional carved-up bench.

"Here?" says Jamie incredulously. "That's pretty stupid."

"No, it's not," says Lily.

"Yes, it is." Jamie waves a hand towards the apartment

building. "No dogs allowed and what do you think they'll see when they look out those windows?"

"But it's the back," says Lily, and I can see she thinks of the apartment building as a head and that the front of the building, where the balconies are, is where the eyes go and consequently is the only part of the building where people will look out. It rather alarms me that I've figured out so quickly what Lily means.

"Come on," you say, and pull Lily forward onto the grass.

I hope that Dog didn't suffer any sort of inner-ear disturbance because her walk made us all dizzy. First she was hauled around the perimeter of the grassy area at top speed, then she was led through a maze of playground obstacles, and finally she was dragged around one of the benches fifty times.

"Exactly fifty times," says Lily, and we all have to count out loud as we traipse behind her.

"Dog abuse," says Jamie, refusing to circle the bench after the twenty-third time.

He sits down on it instead and watches as we sullenly trail after a cheerful Lily. The walk has perked her up considerably.

At the end of the walk, as twilight is falling, we all know a little more about how Lily's brain works, and we are grateful not to have been Dog. In fact, I think we are all glad for Dog, living in the woods and not having to circle a bench fifty times every morning.

"Thank you," I say, but it is the wrong thing to say, and Jamie gives me a look of contempt.

"You're next then, Alice," he says.

To show the others where I used to take Hawk in the early mornings I have to return to the vicinity of the small house

John and I rented. I can't bring myself to go within range because he might be home and we haven't talked since I left. So I start Hawk's walk in the park across the road from the house where I lived. But I'm nervous being here, keep looking back at the small white bungalow with the bed-sheets pinned across the front window in lieu of curtains and the chipped concrete steps with the wobbly wrought-iron railing. Even after so short a time has passed it doesn't look like a place I ever should have lived.

"You lived there with your boyfriend?" you ask.

It is on this walk that you start talking to me, start asking me questions. You ask a disarming number of questions, and I see now how this is a defensive position, how it saves you from having to answer anything someone might want to ask you. But at the time I thought you were genuinely interested in me, and I was flattered and grateful because no one had taken such an interest in me before. And I wanted to know you too. I had so many things I wanted to ask you. But in the end, it all comes down to one question only: What is the worst thing that could have happened if you'd allowed me to love you?

"Yes," I say, leading everyone quickly through the park. "I lived there with my boyfriend."

"For how long?"

"Two years."

"And you don't miss him?"

"Not yet," I say.

Who I really miss at the moment is Hawk. I have done this walk so many times with her that I can feel her beside me, the way a river can feel the current hauling its watery rope towards the sea. If I put my hand down, I think, I could feel the ruff of fur at the back of her neck. I move my hand and it brushes against the back of yours. I look at you. You're looking at me.

This is the moment I could have stepped away from. At

the end it's easy to see what was the beginning and how that beginning could have been avoided. Losing you has been so painful because being with you was so joyful. I never expected to feel that connected to someone, and I never expected to have it taken away so swiftly and completely. And what I don't know how to do is to reconcile those two things. Step away, I would say now. But, of course, I didn't.

We walk through the park towards the river and all I want to do is to hold your hand. Like many North American cities, ours has water at the bottom and woods at the top. We have built our houses between what is fluid and what is fixed. My walk with Hawk in the early mornings was through the park and down to the path that ran along the edge of the river. We would walk to the old factory, where we ran out of path, and then we would walk back home again.

The river is wide where it meets the grassy line of the park. Once I saw a deer swimming frantically in the water here, the whites of its eyes showing and its tawny head barely above the surface. An adult deer. It must have come from farther west, where there is still a smattering of woods between the suburban houses and the golf course. All along this path people stood watching the deer, not realizing that it couldn't scramble onto shore if they were there, that the deer was afraid of them and would rather drown than land among them. I tried to tell several of the people to back away from the edge of the path so the deer would be able to come out of the water, but they wouldn't listen. "We're only watching," they said. "We're not hurting it." I'm sure that the deer did drown, and I'm sure it drowned in full view of that harmless crowd.

I know this walk to the factory as well as I know anything in my life. I have walked it, not just with the dog, but as a teenager, and as a child. As a teenager I came down here at night with friends, heading for the area behind the factory where we would smoke dope and drink beer, our laughter muffled by the waterfall that crashed behind the buildings. As a child I would walk along this path with my mother, on our way to meet my father. We would stand outside the gates of the factory and at five o'clock the doors would open and the men would surge out, just like the waterfall itself, all urgent, forward motion.

Jamie comes up to walk beside me. "Alice," he says, "I think I saw you with your dog here. Was it big and wolfy looking?"

"Yes."

He looks pleased. "Then I did see it," he says. "I used to be down here a lot, skateboarding."

It has seemed to me lately as though Hawk's disappearance equals her death, and I feel hopeful again when Jamie talks about having seen her.

"You must have a good memory," I say.

"I have a good memory for dogs."

We reach the factory. The factory is really several factories, all joined up together. The land was the site of the first sawmill in this area and the original sawmill has been annexed onto the furniture factory itself. A showroom was built and attached to that in the 1930s. The different parts of the building span at least a hundred and fifty years and the building materials show that gap in time. The old sawmill is made of stone. The furniture factory is wood. The showroom is constructed out of brick. They have been joined to one another, not with the straight lines of chronology, but with afterthought, so that the whole structure bulges out in places, overlaps its foundation, and looks like something in the process of exploding apart.

The town grew up around the sawmill and became a small city around the furniture factory. European royalty ate from tables made here, ate from wood cut by the power of this river and planed by the powerful arms of my father.

We stand looking at the factory, and then we turn around. We are walking in groups of three now—Jamie, you, and I up front, Walter Pendleton, Lily, and Malcolm trailing behind.

"There's a good spot for swimming behind the building," says Jamie.

I wonder what I thought about when I walked Hawk. Perhaps I wondered at the vague unhappiness that lay like a film over everything in my life. Perhaps I thought about John and the fact that our feelings for one another probably weren't strong enough to carry us through yet another hard time. Sometimes I thought about moving away to other places where friends lived now. I know that sometimes I didn't think of anything at all, just watched the needles of mist that hung over the river in the early morning, or listened to the roar of the waterfall. Those were always the best mornings, the best walks.

"I fell here once," says Jamie. "And here. And over there. I'm not really very good at skateboarding. Look." He pulls up his pant leg and we stop to admire the ragged scar that trickles down the outside of his knee. "That's the best one."

"Pretty impressive," I say.

The boy is like a dog in that he's constantly stopping to point something out, or to get his bearings by relating an incident that happened to him in a particular place. He's constantly trying to insert himself into the landscape, and I like him for that.

I don't want to get too near to John's house, so I stop the walk in the middle of the park. This is where we would sometimes meet other dogs and Hawk would race around with them for a while before we went home. It was always unpredictable as to whether she would be interested in playing or not. Often she was very aloof from other dogs and would go out of her way to avoid having to play with them.

"That's it," I say, and I stop by the water fountain.

There are some dogs and dog owners here now, over by the children's sandpit. We stand apart from them, watching the dogs tumble after each other in exuberant joy, and the owners speak the clipped shorthand of dog owners everywhere—name of dog, sex, breed, age.

It is strange, watching the group of dogs cavort in the grass at twilight. Dogs that weren't our dogs, but felt as if they should have been. It was as if we were dead. It was as if we were already inhabiting an afterlife.

Later that evening I drive back to the house I shared with John. I have been meaning to come back and collect more of my things and being here today has reminded me of this again.

It is dark. I sit in my car across the street from the small bungalow. The lights are on inside. I can see a shadow move past the bedsheet-curtains. That will be John getting up to fetch another beer or off to the bathroom to pee out the last beer. It depresses me that even though I no longer occupy the same life as he does, I can still predict his movements, that his movements are so few they can be predicted.

I should get out of the car. I should walk up the front steps, knock on the door, and try to engage John in non-hostile banter while I pick up clothes and dishes and the two paintings I like that my friend Ruth did when she was at art college.

But I can't be certain that John won't be hostile, or won't have thrown my stuff out already. I can't be certain that all I'll feel for him will be pity. We slept together for two full years. We ate at the same table—a table he had made for our first anniversary. He was not always the way he is now, and a part of me is angry with myself for not having the patience or willingness to wait around for the old John to reappear.

There are people moving through the park beside where

I'm sitting in the car. I can see their shadows and hear their laughter. Teenagers looking for a place to party.

In the driveway of my old house the motion light comes on and I think that John's come out the side door, that maybe he's seen me, but no one's there. It must have been a cat or a raccoon, walking through the range of light.

John and I had a fight once about that security light. It had burned out and he'd been saying he'd change the bulb for weeks and hadn't, and so I reminded him of this, again, and he went out to do it, angry at me for nagging, and in his anger he forgot to shut off the socket. When he put the new bulb in, it exploded like a blue star and made his arm go numb, and the dog freaked out and ran hard up and down the night grass of the backyard. That's how it was with John and me. The simplest things turned against us. We couldn't seem to make anything work.

I turn the key and start the car. There seems nothing to do now but to drive away.

My shifts at the gas station alternate weekly. One week I'm on mornings—7 a.m. to 3 p.m.—and the next week I'm on evenings—3 p.m. to 11 p.m. The gas station is open twenty-four hours, but the company doesn't allow women to work the midnight shifts. When I was younger, this perceived inequity used to fill me with outrage. Now I am grateful to be spared the drunks and the crazies and the armed robbers.

I quite like the booth that I work in. It's small—desk, chair, safe, credit card machine, racks of maps and oil—but it's snug and comfortable. At night it's unfortunately lit up, and because it's all glass, it glows like a lantern in the middle of the parking lot and attracts people to it like one of those bug lights. But compared to other jobs I've had, and ignoring the low wages, I find working at the gas station fairly benign. I can usually read a book a shift and I can listen to the radio. I can eat whenever I like and I don't have to put up with co-workers. I just have to pump gas, keep the shelves stocked, take the levels in the main tanks once a day, add up the credit card receipts, deposit money whenever there's over two hundred dollars in the till. It's all very manageable.

I have worked at many jobs in my life, and what I have learned from them is what I don't like doing. I don't feel any closer to knowing what I do enjoy.

I have worked in a factory making the plastic bindings that serve as the spines for cookbooks. I have painted houses, delivered mail, stocked shelves. I have worked in the warehouse of a hardware chain, individually pricing screws and hinges. I have worked a shrink-wrap machine, sliding books into a tunnel and having them emerge out the other end wearing a tight corset of hot plastic wrap. I have run a printing press. I have been a proofreader and a typesetter and a paste-up artist. I have delivered catalogues. I have looked after children. I have sat in a sealed room and sent out the emergency services whenever a fire, burglary, or panic alarm was deployed within my area. I have sold insurance. I have sold magazine subscriptions. I have sold chocolate. I have answered phones. I have typed letters and invoices. I have worked in an art storage company. I have been a driver for an automotive parts company.

These are only the jobs I can remember today.

I quit because the boss was hitting on me. I quit because I was about to be fired. I quit because I got frostbite. I quit because the pay was lousy. I quit because I was afraid I was getting asthma from the chemicals. I quit because a toilet fell on my foot and broke my toe. I quit because winter was coming. I quit because summer was coming. I quit because I was sleeping with the boss. I quit because I would never make my quota. I quit because I wanted to go camping with my friends. I quit because I hated it.

Most of the jobs I have done are jobs that other people see as temporary, as jobs for struggling students, as jobs that are beneath most ordinary folk. It has always surprised me how much people buy into appearances, how they don't try to see beyond a uniform or a position. I was never what I did, but over the years I have never been able to become anything else because whenever I try to land something more ambitious, my list of job experiences precludes anyone from taking a chance on me. I can never go to university—as I probably should have done in the beginning, if I hadn't been so desperate to be independent and leave home—because I can never earn enough to save anything in order to go. This financial situation was meant to have changed with John. I agreed to move in with him because he was going to pay the bills and allow me to go to school. This was the big enticement about living with John. When he had been employed and feeling good about himself, he was a generous man. He certainly wasn't the worst boyfriend I've ever had.

I had a boyfriend who raced stock cars. I had a boyfriend who built a wall in his basement out of empty beer bottles. I had a boyfriend who could bench-press two hundred and twenty. I had a boyfriend who could do calligraphy. I had a boyfriend who took four showers a day. I had a boyfriend who had a boyfriend. I had a boyfriend who spoke in tongues.

I left him because he couldn't read. I left him because he was alcoholic and the sex was not worth the effort. I left him because he made this annoying smacking sound when he ate. I left him because he was the hero in all his stories. I left him because I wanted to sleep with someone else. I left him because it was lonelier to be with him than to be without him. I left him because I didn't love him.

It's funny, but the job I remember the clearest is the job

that started it all—the car wash. I worked there for two years, from the age of seventeen to nineteen, and it set the pattern, not only for my choice of jobs, but for how I was treated in the jobs I had.

My job at the car wash was to stand inside the car-wash tunnel between the rinse arch and the dryers. A car would nose through the mist, propelled along by a roller behind the front wheel, and I would vault into the interior, wash the inside front window, side windows, wipe the dash, replace the floor mats—then drive the car the hundred yards out to the street. I would leap out and race back up the tunnel for the next car. If it was sunny, we could wash seven hundred cars a day. I drove them all as if they were mine.

Inside the tunnel, cars plodded as stupid as old trail horses along a track solemn with rust. On good days I was some kind of weird intergalactic cowgirl, poised beneath the rinse arch, stale water frisking around my head, waiting to leap into the soft leather saddle of a Mercedes or Rolls or airport limousine. Brushes gyrated, plastic skirts lifted in the steam and stagnant water. On bad days I stood under the fetid spray of the rinse arch and knew I wasn't getting out of there.

Already the idea of university was diffusing. Already my friends were a year ahead of me and I didn't see them much any more. I couldn't go to their parties because I had to get up at four-thirty in the morning. I couldn't talk theory about the books I read. My hands were red and chapped from being wet all day and my skin always smelled embarrassingly of carnauba wax. This wax is used on both cars and candies, gives them a nice, shiny coating.

No one had to be nice to me. That's what I learnt at the car wash. I wasn't protected by anything. Even the total slimeball who worked at the car-rental agency down the street could accuse me of stealing loose change from his ashtray and be believed. It didn't matter that I was reading all the books on the university English list. What mattered was that working at the car wash was lower than almost everything else, and somehow everyone knew this.

There was always the sound of water at the car wash. The hiss of water in the drains. The steady drip of the brushes. It was as if it was forever raining indoors, and I grew to hate that, as I grew to hate the smell of the spray I cleaned the windows with, how it burned into my lungs and made me gasp for breath.

There was often disaster at the car wash. Sometimes a car would be left in drive and, engine on, it would pick up speed as it journeyed down the tunnel, hurtle forward along the metal track, jumping the rollers. The only way to stop it would be to drop the industrial doors at the end of the tunnel but the car would plough spectacularly through them, a crescendo of glass exploding the air. It would sometimes fly right out onto the road and hit another car. There would be the sound of metal tearing and the skew of twisted chrome on the asphalt; people getting out of their cars to have a look.

Those of us who worked at the car wash would watch all this happening, stand perfectly still and watch the car rush by us while the owner ran screaming through the tunnel. *Do something! Do something!* But we knew there was nothing to be done. This was the lesson of working at the car wash. All the men I worked with were living lives they hadn't expected and didn't really want. They knew, and I was learning, that if something has momentum behind it, it cannot be stopped.

There was a small laundromat next door to the car wash. I remember it well because it was always so mysterious. No one ever seemed to go in and out with dirty or clean clothes, and yet the machines were always running. In summer, when the door was open, I could hear the mechanical drone of the dryers. Sometimes they made a loud rattling sound, as though they were all full of loose change.

The old man who ran the laundromat would sit outside in the good weather and smoke. He never read or talked on the phone. He just sat on a low wooden bench, his back pressed against the concrete wall of the building, and he smoked cigarette after cigarette.

One day I was at the car wash early because I'd agreed to clean and wax a car. Because we were always so busy in the day, this individual service had to be performed before the car wash opened.

It was a spring morning and I had the industrial doors at the front of the building open to let in the warm May air. I heard the man next door drive his truck up to the laundromat, and I watched as he unloaded plastic pails from the back of the truck and staggered each one into the building. I could see that what was in the pails was pink in colour. Since it took the man a while to emerge from the laundromat after he'd lugged a pail inside, I wandered over and looked into the back of his truck.

The pails were full of pink triangles of flesh, bloody and with coarse blond hairs still stuck to them. Pigs' ears. They'd been cut off the pig neatly. The edges were clean. Maybe they'd used garden shears or a large, sharp knife. The sound I could hear in the dryers, that sound like loose change, was the sound of the pigs' ears drying out, drying into dog chews.

It is on Walter Pendleton's walk that I realize a fundamental truth about the six of us. We gather across the street from the tidy brick house where Walter lives with his daughter, son-in-law, and their new baby.

"The baby will be sleeping," says Walter, rather gloomily. "We have to get into the car without alerting anyone."

We look at the station wagon parked in the driveway of the brick house. Four doors have to open and close. An engine has to cough into life. It seems unlikely we will get away undetected. And that's when it occurs to me—we're all afraid of the people we live with, the ones who gave our dogs away. If we weren't afraid of them, they wouldn't have had the authority to do what they did.

"You get the car," says Jamie. "And we'll wait down the block for you."

Walter walks furtively up his driveway, and we scuttle down the street and congregate by the mailbox, feeling as if we are participating in a bank robbery. When the car approaches we dash out into the road and clamber into the interior, slamming the doors in unison. Walter is breathless. He wipes his brow with the chamois leather shoved down the pocket in the car door. He is overweight and wearing what looks like a pyjama top. Everywhere that his shirt touches his skin is damp with sweat.

Georgie's walk is really a drive. We drive around the neighbourhood and Walter points out all the other houses that contain dogs, and what sort of dogs they contain. Mr. Pendleton divides dogs up into two categories—nice and nasty. There seem to be more nasty specimens than nice ones where he lives. We get onto the main road and drive past a few brightly lit strip plazas. Mr. Pendleton points out a bakery. "Georgie likes their sausage rolls," he says.

The car makes Lily nervous. She starts humming and rocking back and forth in her seat. "Where are we?" she says every couple of minutes, and we all ignore her question after responding the first few times. Only Walter consistently tries to find a calming answer for her. "We're not far," he says, turning around from his position in the front seat and then having to swerve quickly back into his lane.

Lily, you, and I sit squashed together in the back seat of the station wagon. Jamie has scrambled into the very back, and even though it's grubby and smells like dog back there, he has the most room.

"Why did they get rid of your dog?" he shouts from the back. We're driving past a row of used-car dealers. The sun is setting above the flags in the parking lot.

Walter Pendleton keeps both hands on the wheel and speaks so softly into the windshield that I have to turn in my seat and repeat the answer for Jamie.

"His daughter was afraid the dog would hurt the baby," I say.

I can feel you sitting beside me on the back seat of the station wagon. I can feel the muscles in your leg that press against mine. I can feel the wiry length of your arm tucked in beside my ribs. I try to concentrate on what people are saying in the car, or what's going by outside the window, but eventually I give this up. On one side of me Lily rocks back and forth in nervous agitation and on the other side of me I can feel the heat blossom on your skin.

Walter Pendleton parks the car by the old train station. The train doesn't come to this town any more and the old wooden station is overgrown with weeds, broken-windowed and spray-painted with gang graffiti. We pile out of the car and stand on the ground by the boarded-up entrance. Pieces of beer-bottle glass grind down under my shoes.

"There are rats here," says Walter Pendleton. "Georgie liked rats."

"Rats and sausage rolls," you say quietly to me.

We walk along the rails. Freight trains still go through here and the rails are smooth and oily like the barrel of a gun. I bend down and put my hand on the steel, feel where it has been touched by the last of the sun.

"Why are you always sad?" you say from above me, and I don't answer because I think I've misheard you, and yet I can't decide what it really was you did say. When I stand up you've walked on ahead and there's just Lily waiting for me, all agitated and jumpy.

"I think the train's coming," she says.

"We'd hear it," I say.

"I think it's coming," she says again, "and it will run us down." All of us are walking within the margin of the rails.

"It's not coming," I say.

Lily is always afraid, I think. She's always afraid that she doesn't understand what's going on, or that she is the only one who does. Always there is danger. Always she has to flee the burning building. She's never able to be at ease. And perhaps you're right. Perhaps I am always sad. How would I know?

"It's all right, baby," I say to Lily. I reach out and take her hand. "I've got you."

I used to wonder if you really had a wolf dog. You had no pictures of Lopez, no evidence that you'd come home from your work in the woods with a wolf pup. Sometimes I used to think that you were the wolf. You even looked like a wolf, with your thin, lanky body and the high planes of your face.

Now I can see how many wolf characteristics you had. You were wary, didn't really trust anyone or anything. You were elusive and secretive. You paced out behind the trees, watching everything and waiting for the moment when it was safe to come in and rest by the fire. But you weren't happy there—no, I take that back, you were happy there, but you weren't comfortable. It wasn't what you knew. It wasn't what you trusted. You trusted meanness, not kindness. Kindness spooked you—you were always looking for the trap in it. You trusted in a scrappy existence where you had to fight for your survival.

So why did you love me? For I believe that you did. I have to believe that you did, for my own sanity. Maybe you dreamed that you could leave the shelter of the trees and come in by the fire. Or perhaps that was just my dream for you.

Every day, at four o'clock, six deer step from the woods and graze on the tall grass by the stream. From the cabin where I write this, I can watch their cautious parade between the trees. They are never more than a few minutes either side of four o'clock. I marvel at this innate punctuality and I wonder too if wildness, on some level, is also control. Is the pattern of the deer, the pattern of the birds that sing at dawn, the pattern of the spawning fish, part of nature's rhythm of survival?

The deer stay for half an hour at the stream. They bend their long necks into the marshy grasses by the water's edge. There are coins of light on their backs from where the sun has slipped through the leaves overhead. Once they have decided it is safe to step out from the trees, that there is no danger at the stream, they are no longer afraid, and when they are no longer afraid I can see how vulnerable they are. There is something very sweet, very tender, in the gesture of lowering their heads to nudge at the wisps of marshy grasses. They trust the world completely in that instant, and I can see how their enormous fear is equally balanced by this capacity to trust in their surroundings, and there is peace in that, and I wish that were possible for you.

Jamie used to run Scout alongside his bicycle. "But I can't do that with you," he says to the five of us. "You couldn't keep up."

Instead, he takes us to a small, stony beach on the river that is reached by walking through marshland. The ground is spongy and the cattails are over our heads. Every few feet there is a broken shopping cart or an old tire. The beach itself is strewn with debris from the river—tampon applicators, plastic bottles, a yellow rubber glove, pellets of Styrofoam.

"This is where my father used to bring me," says Jamie, and I almost ask why, but I stop myself in time. The little beach is certainly not one of the more scenic places around. It looks out onto the muddy channel at the wide part of the river and an opposite shore choked with new suburban homes. It is difficult to access and too small to walk along.

"When?" I ask.

"When I was five."

We gingerly pick our way to the water's edge and look across to the houses with their large decks of pre-treated lumber, their enormous barbecues, their tubs of pink geraniums.

"Those houses weren't there," says Jamie. "Nothing was here. And this beach didn't have all this garbage on it." He picks up a rock and flings it, hard, out over the span of water. He has thrown it so far, we don't hear the splash. "My father swam here every morning," he says finally. "That's why we came down here. He swam across to the other side and back again, and I sat over there." He points to a big willow tree by the water's edge. "I waited there and I made a wall with the stones. Piled them up around me. And I watched my father's arms in the water. Away from me and then back again."

I look out over the channel and I can almost see the swimmer's arms lift up and down in the water, see his return to the beach. I remember going with my mother to meet my own father at the factory. How excited I was to see him. How he would swing me overhead and carry me home on his shoulders.

"What happened to your father?" I ask Jamie, remembering that it was his stepfather who sent his dog away.

The boy kicks at the stones on the beach, doesn't look at me. "He left when I was six. I haven't seen him again."

I can still imagine the swimmer, the water churning around his body, the flash of his arms hooking through the air. There is always a leaving before the leaving, I think. There is a moment when the rope goes slack. Jamie's father practised moving away from him and then coming back until he could allow himself to just move away. Perhaps even Hawk knew she was leaving when she decided to sleep downstairs on the couch instead of upstairs on my bed. There is a moment when the rope goes slack and it is the most frightening moment of all for the ones who are about to be left.

"Where are we?" says Lily. She has wandered back up towards the marsh, turns to face us in a panic. I wonder at the wisdom of her parents in letting her out of the house at all. Or perhaps they are hoping something will happen to her.

Jamie straightens his shoulders, jams his hands into the front pockets of his jeans. "Nowhere," he says.

You don't take us on a dog walk either. "I never went to the same place twice," you say. "There would be no point."

You take us back to your rented apartment near the university and you show us slides of the wolf pack you're studying in the woods north of here.

The apartment is a sublet and I'm relieved to find this out because I don't want to believe that you're the sort of person who collects the piles of shells, coated with dust, that cover all the window ledges in the apartment. I don't want to believe you would have macramé holders for your hanging plants or cute pictures of cats in the bathroom. When I ask you where you really live, you just smile and push me down onto the couch beside Lily. You hang a bedsheet from

the bookcase to make a screen for the slides and you pull
the curtains on the windows, turn off the lights.

You show slides of the wolves in the pack you're studying,
explain who is the alpha male and the alpha female, who is
the offspring of whom. The wolves gaze balefully out at us,
yellow eyes shrewd and cold, their scrawny frames matted
with knots of fur.

"Wolves don't alter their environment," you say. "They
won't make cover by digging a den, but rather they will use
what is already there—a hollow tree, a cave in a cliff."

"Dogs do that too," I say, although I have known Hawk to
try to dig a hole in order to shelter from an approaching
storm. Is that sort of opportunism a symptom of wildness
or civility? Is opportunism innate or adaptive? I ask you
that and you're silent for a moment. A slight breeze blows
into the room from the window and the image of the wolf
on the bedsheet lifts and settles like breath.

"I don't know," you say.

There's the dry hum of the projector in the room and the
noise of Lily squirming on the couch beside me. I feel very
satisfied to have asked you a question that you can't
answer and I can tell that it bothers you not to have an
answer because you forget to change the slide. The wolf
on the bedsheet moves up and down with the breeze from
the window.

"I saw a wolf kill once," I say. Now that I've started trying
to impress you I can't seem to stop myself from continuing.
"It was winter and I was visiting a friend who was spending
that year in a cottage on the edge of a lake. We skied out
across the frozen lake one afternoon and found a deer lying
on the ice in a little bay."

"What was it like?" says Jamie. "Was there lots of blood?"

"On the snow, yes, but the deer was picked pretty clean.
We found the head on shore, behind some trees. The

wolves must have driven the deer out onto the ice so they had a clearer run at it."

I remembered that there were wing-prints near the carcass, like brush strokes of calligraphy. "There were birds feeding too. I saw the pattern of their wings in the snow."

"Ravens," you say. "They have a special relationship with wolves. Often they will lead wolves to a carcass because they need the wolves to tear the flesh before they can feed."

I remembered the trampled snow around the body of the deer and how my friend and I had made a story up about what happened. The wolves had run the deer out onto the ice and killed her. They had fought amongst themselves over feeding order because the snow was stuck with tufts of fur and there was as much piss around the carcass as blood.

The room is quiet and still except for the slight breeze at the window and the sound of Lily shuffling on the couch. We're all watching the wolf lift and fall, lift and fall, as though he is alive and breathing here, in the midst of us.

"It was very dramatic," I say. "I mean, you could still feel the drama. You could smell it in the air." It was like the frisson that accompanies sex, but I don't say this. "Excitement," I say instead. "The air was charged with excitement."

There is a silence, and when you speak I know you are speaking directly to me.

"At the kill, a wolf will go for the soft organs first," you say. "The lungs. The liver."

You pause and I can feel a certain apprehension because I know what you will say next.

"The heart."

When it's time for us to leave and we're on the stairs outside the apartment, you pull me back inside and tell the others to go on ahead.

We're standing in the hallway by the coats. There's a postcard from Mexico pinned above the light switch.

"I wanted to tell you something." You've got your hand on my arm and I am both reassured and alarmed by this gesture.

"What?" I say.

"There's something that can't be figured out about wolves," you say. "No one knows why they choose one animal over another to kill. A wolf will sometimes be staring down a deer, will have run the deer, separated it out from the herd, and be ready to kill it, and then, at the last minute, the wolf will change its mind, release the deer and go off and choose another deer to kill.

"What they think happens," you say, "is that the wolf has a conversation of death with its prey."

"What does that mean?"

"The wolf asks the deer if it's willing to die, enters into a sort of telepathic courtship with it, assesses its will to live, and based on the information it receives, decides to kill the deer or spare it."

"Like the victim agreeing to be the victim," I say.

"Exactly." You take your hand from my arm and then I take your hand and hold onto it.

"A conversation of death," I say. "Just like we're having." Only we both know that I mean a conversation of love.

Malcolm is nervous about having the others come onto his property. He wants to start his dog walk on the other side of the stream from the cabin where I'm staying, but he doesn't let anyone drive down the driveway past the farmhouse.

"My mother will be alarmed," he says, by way of explanation.

I have begun to doubt that he has a mother. In the time I've been living in the cabin I have yet to see any evidence of Malcolm's mother. Malcolm himself has bothered me less than I'd anticipated. He sometimes leaves utensils or items he thinks I might need on the front porch by the door for me, but he rarely knocks or wants to talk.

"I don't think he has a mother," I say to you, as we're crashing through the woods to avoid having to go near the farmhouse. "I've never seen her."

"He seems harmless enough."

"What do you know?" I say. "You live with wolves."

You hold a pine branch aside so I can pass. "Look, if you're really worried, you don't have to stay there."

But when you see the cabin you are as enchanted by it as I have become. You walk around the outside, looking at the old chinking between the logs, the axe marks on the wood, each rough square made by someone's living swing, arms overhead and then the stroke down towards the ground.

"I could help you reshingle the roof," you say. "It looks like it leaks."

"It does leak." Even though Malcolm has lent me several buckets to place beneath the drips, there are more leaks than buckets.

"It's like a hideout," says Jamie, who has caught up to us. He goes in and out several times, banging the rickety screen door behind him. "Cool," he says, each time he comes back out again.

Malcolm scoots around the side of the cabin, beckons us to follow him across the stream. For some reason he's not talking. Does he really think his (fictional) mother will hear him all the way out here? Even if she did exist and have perfect hearing, the cabin is too far from the farmhouse for her to be able to make out our voices or the noise of us splashing through the stream.

There are stones placed a foot apart to use as a bridge to cross the stream, but we get our feet wet anyway.

"What's he doing?" hisses Jamie from behind me. I look

up and see Malcolm on the other side of the stream, making urgent waves with his hands.

"He's stopped talking," I say.

Jamie lurches onto the same rock as me, steadies himself by grabbing onto the back of my shirt.

"It's too bad you don't still have your dog," he says, and I know that he means out here, in the cabin, to protect me from the potential lunacy of Malcolm.

The woods that lie across the stream from my cabin are the same woods that join up with the woods behind Cooper's farm. It is easy to see how Sidney, once free to roam through here, followed the scent of the other dogs and left to join up with them.

We stumble between the trees. Malcolm leaps up ahead like some kind of forest nymph and is soon lost to view. You walk ahead with Lily. I walk with Jamie, and Walter Pendleton trails cautiously behind all of us, occasionally swearing as he trips over a root or a stone.

"I do have better things to do," says Jamie, as we're struggling over a fallen birch and trying not to get poked by all the dead branches.

"Like what?" Up ahead I can hear Lily ask you where we are.

"Skateboarding. Hanging out with my friends." He kicks at the rotten tree and successfully knocks off several of the smaller branches.

"I thought you weren't that good at skateboarding."

"I'm improving."

"Then why are you here?" I ask, before he can ask me if I don't have better things to do.

Jamie stops on the other side of the birch. His hair is mussed and he has a scratch on his left cheek just below his eye. His jeans are filthy and his shirt is untucked. "I miss my dog," he says. "I want him back."

And of course this is why he is here, why we're all here,

because doing this, going on these walks, is about our dogs, is connected to them, is the step we can take in faith towards their imagined return.

"I know," I say, for I feel the same.

And later, when I think about you, that is also what I feel. Everything else falls away—the difficulties, the bad way it ended between us, all the words that were said and never said. It feels very simple now, what I'm left with, what remains. I miss you. I want to see you again.

We catch up to you and Lily, walk behind you on the path. Behind me I can hear the heavy breathing of Walter Pendleton. There is still no sign of Malcolm bouncing up ahead through the trees.

It is that time of day when the late sun casts a gold net over everything and the different shades of green glow with a deep resonance, as though the light sounds from some-where inside them. This is my favourite time of day, these moments before dark seeps through the hours, when the light goes down blazing, all hands on deck. I want to ask you if you like this too, but you're talking to Lily, so instead I say to Jamie, "Look how green it all is."

"Of course it's green," he says, scowling at me as though I've lost my mind. "They're trees. Trees are green."

Then you turn around. "Look at the light," you say. "Isn't it beautiful?"

We get lost in the woods. Malcolm is waiting for us by a moss-covered boulder. He has twigs in his hair and seems to have recovered his voice. "I don't know where we are," he says.

"What do you mean?" I ask.

"I mean, I'm lost." Malcolm scuffs his foot on the forest floor and flattens several mushrooms. "Usually the dog leads me out when we go back here for a walk."

"Asshole," says Jamie under his breath, but loud enough for me to hear.

Lily starts to whimper and you put your arm around her. "You could make a trail, Malcolm," you say, rather wearily.

"I don't need a trail when I have the dog," he says.

"Asshole," says Jamie, again.

It's dark by the time we struggle out of the woods. You lead us back towards the stream and we do get there, although I don't think it's by the route we came initially. You leave to drive Lily and Jamie home and I sit with Walter Pendleton on the front porch of the cabin while he rests up enough to make the journey back to his car. Malcolm, humiliated by the experience of getting lost, has wisely scurried off to his house.

"It was an adventure and an ordeal," says Walter Pendleton. "And I think my ankles are swollen."

I don't say anything. I feel cranky that I didn't really get to say goodbye to you and I just want Walter Pendleton to leave before he asks me to tend to any of his health complaints. I have already heard about his scrapes and bug bites and the fact that he is waiting for a cataract operation.

"You'll feel better when you're home having your supper," I say finally, and at the mention of food he allows me to lead him out to the road where his car is parked.

I stand at the side of the road, watching the tail lights of Walter Pendleton's station wagon disappear around the bend. The stars wire the sky together and the crickets fill the shadows on the earth with their breath. I'm thinking of supper, about whether to open a can of tuna or a can of beans, and I stand there long enough to feel the cool mist of evening rise up from the ground and drape itself around me, to hear the cry of an owl crawl out over the dark, to realize that what I feel for you is getting stronger with every passing moment.

When I get back to the cabin I've decided on tuna, open the can, and mix it up with curry paste and celery to make a sandwich. I'm doing this when there is a knock on the door and you're standing on the front porch.

"I didn't really say goodbye," you say. You're talking to me through the broken screen door.

I have lit the kerosene lamp and made my supper. The cabin looks cosy and clean. "Come in and have something to eat," I say, standing on the other side of the screen door.

"That would be dangerous."

Danger is not how I'm thinking of it. I push open the screen door and it creaks on its one good hinge, and you hesitate for a moment, and then you step into the cabin.

Once I knew I loved you, before I actually told you, there was no stopping me. It was as if I hadn't realized how empty I'd been, as if there had always been a black wire of loneliness twisting in my guts. I had never felt with anyone what I felt with you, and I still believe in that, despite all that's happened.

Love is momentum and love is opportunism. I can see that now, how I rode through the moments of it with a kind of cavalier optimism. I never doubted it, only wanted more of it, more of being with you.

You helped me fix the roof on the cabin and I liked how easily we worked together. Using my body always calms my mind, takes away the anxiety that lies like a sheet over everything I think and feel. Working suited you too and I liked the rhythm we had between us, how we worked until we got the job done and how we were both exhausted but happy.

While we worked on the cabin we talked about the missing dogs.

"Do you think the stories are true?" I ask. There was an account in the papers last week that said a woman had been mauled by the wild dogs when she approached them on the road near the city dump. She had stopped her car and walked towards the pack. The dogs had tried to rip her throat out. She only escaped because another car stopped and the driver managed to beat the dogs back with a tire jack. There was a photo of the woman in hospital, her face criss-crossed with stitches, bandages covering her neck and chest.

"That the dogs will attack us if we try to go near them?" You put your hammer down and wipe your forehead with the back of your hand. "I don't know."

"Aren't they still ours?" The papers have warned against going into the woods to reclaim our lost pets. *They quickly turn wild*, the article had said.

"Were they ever ours? Maybe what passed for being tame was simply opportunism. Shelter. Food. A warm place to sleep."

You look so good, sitting on the cabin roof in the sun, and what I want to say, but don't dare say, is, *Aren't you mine?*

The six of us still wait every evening at the edge of the woods behind the fields of Cooper's farm. It is rare now that we see the dogs. They don't break from the trees and run across the fields as they used to. Sometimes we catch a glimpse of white fur flashing by inside the bars of the woods and we are hopeful, but usually there's nothing to see, nothing to hear. Perhaps the dogs have chosen another exit point, or perhaps they've chosen another time of day to make their forays into the outside world. We have nothing to go on but what we once knew, and as the days go by, we find that knowledge no longer serves us.

It is hard to have faith, for that is what we require now. Knowing is easy, belief is difficult. Knowledge is tangible. Faith is reach, and some of us just can't do it.

I have forgotten what Hawk looks like. She has been gone for weeks now and I have forgotten the way she moves, the look in her eyes when she sees me. I have forgotten the sound of her bark and the exact shadings of her coat.

So what have I hung onto? I have hung onto the idea that the moment I see Hawk again all knowledge of her will come flooding back. This thin cord of belief stretches between what I have lost and what is perhaps retrievable. So much depends on the notion that I will see the dog again, that our connection will be renewed.

Jamie cannot muster the same faith. There is an end to his waiting. One day in late August he flings his bike down on the grass and walks quickly up and down in front of the trees, as usual, but this time he doesn't call out his dog's name. He paces for a few moments and then he comes over to me.

"They're gone," he says. His face is red in an effort to keep from crying.

"No," I say. "They're in there. We know that."

"Gone," he says again. "We're not getting them back."

I want to put my arm around him, but I sense he wouldn't like this, so I don't. We look at each other while I struggle to think of something reassuring to say.

"Be careful." He nods his head towards Malcolm. "Of him. And of her." He looks at you, bent over and explaining something to Lily at the edge of the trees.

"What do you mean?" I ask, but Jamie is already moving away from me. He picks his bike up and rides off without a backwards glance, wheels wobbling against the rutted earth of the field.

He doesn't come back. He's not there the next evening or the one after that. He just disappears back into that life he occupied before I met him. I miss him more than I had expected, and I'm always listening for the sound of his bike riding up behind me.

After Jamie has gone I'm less interested in coming out to the woods, although I still do it because the others do and I don't want to break that pattern. But now I want both Jamie and Hawk to come back and some evenings that feels a little unbearable. But two things happen in the following week that make me glad I continued the vigil.

The five of us stand at the edge of the woods one Tuesday evening. This is after Jamie has gone. We no longer call out for the dogs now. It has been days since we've seen them and there seems no point, although we can't quite give up the act of waiting. It is the only thing that keeps the space open between the dogs and us.

We are waiting at the edge of the woods. It is a cool evening. The wind stirs the grasses in the field behind us, pushing through in a restless surge. I can feel the wind at the back of my neck like breath.

We are standing apart from one another. You are the closest person to me, and you are at least a hundred feet away. We often stand like this now, all strung out as though we are lights on a cord, pulled tight against the trunks of the pines at the edge of the woods. Lily is at one end of the line, two people away from me, and so it is easy to ignore her. I spend less time with her the more time I spend with you. But I do see her lift her hand and wave, and I lift my hand and wave back, and then she is gone. Most evenings Lily is driven home by you or me, but she might have decided to take the bus tonight. She sometimes does. She has been discouraged since Jamie left, thinks now that the dogs won't come back, and she often wants to leave the woods before the rest of us do.

I waved my hand to Lily and I thought, oh, she's going home now, and then I forgot all about her. Now, of course, knowing that I will never see Lily again, I wish I'd shown more interest in her that evening. I wish I'd not let my connection to her slip in my eagerness to attach myself to you. But I forget about Lily's whereabouts moments after she's gone because of the second thing that happens that evening. One of the dogs comes out of the woods. It is Walter Pendleton's Jack Russell, Georgie. He comes out from the shelter of the trees, noticeably limping, his coat dirty and stuck through with pine needles. We all stare at him, not believing that he is real, and then Walter Pendleton rushes forward.

"Georgie!" he says, and Georgie holds up his left front paw and wags his tail weakly.

We all crowd around the dog as though he has returned from battle and will tell us the news of our fallen comrades. He looks up at us obligingly, but there is nothing to be gleaned from his expression. He is thinner than he should be, and that does tell us something about how the pack is faring. Georgie is only a small dog and doesn't need much to eat; surely this means that the larger dogs aren't surviving as well.

"I hope none of them have died," you say, and then, "Watch it," because Walter Pendleton has bent down to lift Georgie up into his arms. "He might still be wild."

But Georgie willingly hops up into his master's arms, looking like nothing more than an injured pet. Did he choose to come back? I wonder. Or was he banished by the other, uninjured dogs? Was he ever wild, or was he simply enjoying an outing with his kind? Unfortunately, Georgie isn't giving anything away. He settles into the sling of Walter Pendleton's arms, groans contentedly, and falls asleep.

"Well," says Walter, after a short, rather awkward silence. "I suppose I'll be going then." For to get one's dog back surely means that his time here with the rest of us is done, that he no longer has a right to the long wait out here at dusk.

"Goodbye, then," we all say, as Walter Pendleton and Georgie head off through the field towards where his car is parked.

"That's hopeful," says Malcolm, and we do feel optimistic

about Georgie's return. If one dog came back, certainly another might. Malcolm, you, and I stay longer than usual at the edge of the woods, stay well after dark, waiting for another dog to break from the cover of the trees and return to us. But not one of them does.

It is only the next evening, when we are gathered out here again and Lily is absent, that we begin to wonder at her disappearance. Lily has never missed an evening at the woods. I suspect it is the highlight of her day.

The first night she isn't there we remark on it. The second night we start to worry. The third night what we fear is confirmed.

Walter Pendleton rejoins us at the edge of the woods. He must have hurried over from his car as his face is red and he's panting quite heavily.

"She's missing," he says, when he catches up to us. "Lily. She's gone missing. They had it on the news last night. I think we should call the police."

"What did they say?" I ask.

Walter pulls a crumpled handkerchief from his trouser pocket and pats his forehead with it. "I need some water," he says. "I think I might be suffering from dehydration."

He's really suffering from being out of shape and a little hysterical as far as his health is concerned. I remember the horribly boring conversation I had with him about his filmy eyes.

"Malcolm," I say. "Could we go to your house and have a cup of tea or something?"

Malcolm looks panicked. "My mother," he says quickly, "she'll be resting."

We go back to the cabin instead. I fetch Walter a glass of water and make tea for the rest of us. We sit out on the front porch in the shade of the pines that grow beside the cabin. The air is hot and still and there is a temporary lull in insect activity. It is the changing of the guard from deerflies to mosquitoes and there is usually a half-hour intermission every evening when this takes place.

"Well?" you say, after Walter has sucked back most of his glass of water. "What did you hear about Lily?"

"Her name is Lily Steadman," says Walter. "Did we know that?"

"No." I realize how little we know of one another. I only know Walter's and Malcolm's last names because they introduced themselves to me that way.

"Her name is Lily Steadman," continues Walter, "and I have to say that I don't think much of her parents. They said that she's always suffered and perhaps she wandered off to kill herself. Her mother even uttered the words 'God's will.'" He finishes his glass of water and puts the empty glass down beside him on the porch. "It's a little embarrassing," he says.

"What is?" you say.

"Well," says Walter, "they think she might have been abducted by her boyfriend."

"What boyfriend?" says Malcolm.

"Exactly." Walter stretches his legs out and I can see his white ankles puffing out around the tops of his short brown socks. "It seems that Lily disappears every evening, goes off to meet someone, and they think this person may have taken her."

We're all silent for a moment while we consider what Walter has just said.

"But if we tell the police there is no boyfriend, they might come out here and go into the woods to look for her. And wouldn't they," says Malcolm, "shoot the dogs if they came upon them?"

"She could be in the woods," I say. "Maybe she didn't go home as we thought but went into the woods."

"I thought that," says Walter. "I did. When I first saw the

story on the news. Lily doesn't like to go new places. Why would she just wander off somewhere? She doesn't like not knowing where she is."

"We should probably say something," you say. "But before we tell the truth about the boyfriend, maybe we should go into the woods ourselves."

"Shouldn't we call the police?" I say. The thought of Lily wandering lost for three days has made me afraid for her survival.

You don't answer right away. "Well," you say after a while, "if we call the police, there'll be a lot of time wasted with all their questions. Wouldn't it be easier if we just settled the matter for ourselves?"

I don't agree with this, but I don't say anything. It has surprised me that you care less for Lily than for your need to control the situation. But then I think that maybe, if Lily is in the woods, we will have a better chance of finding her. She would be afraid of the police and might hide from them.

We decide to search the following day.

Malcolm has taken to visiting me in the evenings, and I have taken to spying on him at night. When I'm working mornings I'm finished by three. Usually I run errands in the afternoon, buy groceries, do laundry, and then I meet you and Malcolm at the woods at dusk. After that I go back to the cabin and have supper. Sometimes you come with me, but more often than not you come over much later and stay the night. What happens most days is that I have my supper in the cabin, and then when I leave it to get water from the stream, or to walk in the woods before dark, or to fetch something from the car, I find Malcolm sitting on the cabin steps. He never knocks at the door, but he is obviously there for me. On the nights when I'm not home, or when I don't come out of the cabin, I imagine he sits out there waiting for a certain amount of time anyway and then trots back to his house.

I cannot figure Malcolm Dodd out. I don't know exactly what he wants from me, but I do know he wants something.

He will sit on the cabin steps and I will go out and sit beside him. If I offer him something, a cup of coffee or tea, a beer, he will always refuse. We will sit there for a while, not saying anything, and then he will talk. There is no small talk with Malcolm. It is as though he just opens his mouth and the long ribbon of thought that is twisting through his mind unravels out into speech instead.

Tonight Malcolm is full of questions. I take a mug of coffee out with me, sit beside him on the cabin steps. He is flaking off bits of rotten wood with his thumbnail, looks nervously up at me and then back down at the steps again.

We talk about Lily's disappearance for a bit, and then he says, "Do you think the dogs wanted to be wild?"

"Wanted to?"

"As if they were always waiting for the opportunity. That they were just biding their time with us."

"Couldn't they be one thing and then another?" I say, but I know what he means. It is easier to think that the dogs were simply deceiving us than to believe that they could entirely change.

"Is it in us, then?" says Malcolm.

"I don't know."

The shadows are lengthening around the cabin. It looks as if all the trees are lying down on the forest floor, each one pillowed on a cushion of moss.

"I think it might be in us," I say finally. "And that's what we are afraid of."

Malcolm is silent and I think that I have scared him. I try and think of something reassuring to say, but can't.

"I don't like this place," he says. "I've never liked it."

"You could leave."

"Can't do that. Not now." He flicks a piece of rotten wood off the step. "I used to want to be a painter," he says after a moment.

I had a job once in an art gallery. At night, when everyone had left and all the lights were turned off, I would run through the long galleries, vault the padded leather benches. I wanted to experience the paintings as movement instead of stasis. They had been movement once, colours whirling at the end of the painter's arm, and it was surprising how different they appeared when I ran them down. It was never completely dark in the gallery. There was always light from outside and the reflected white of the walls. The paintings would flash by, reds flickering like flame at the side of my vision, blacks stringing together a rope of darkness. Movement makes everything abstract. Even the stiffest portrait will bleed into a pool of colour if you race past it. And this is the strange thing, perhaps, because a painting is intended to stop a moment.

I say this to Malcolm, how I ran through the gallery at night, how the action worked against the intention of the painters who had fashioned the art.

Malcolm stops picking at the wood on the steps. He looks out into the darkening forest. "That's not right," he says. "A painting doesn't stop a moment. It resolves it."

Malcolm always leaves just before the woods go completely dark, just before night extinguishes the last sallow spill of light between the trees. He leaves and I wait at least half an hour and then I creep over to the farmhouse and spy on him. I know the woods so well now that I don't need a flashlight to guide me along the path between the cabin and the farmhouse, and once I get to the farmhouse I follow the interior lights, moving outside from window to window as Malcolm moves inside from room to room.

The farmhouse is a mess. There are piles of old newspapers everywhere. There are empty jars and cans piled into the corners of the rooms. In one of the rooms there are several mirrors stacked against one wall. Malcolm moves from place to place, touching objects and talking out loud, flipping the lights on and then off again. He seems agitated and entirely lacking in purpose.

Spying on Malcolm has taught me two important things about him. The first thing is that the disorder of the farmhouse must find an echo in the disorder of his mind. And the second, more important piece of information is that there is no one else living with Malcolm Dodd in that farmhouse. His mother, if she did exist, does not live there now.

I think about the person who made my cabin. At night I lie in bed and look across at the opposite wall, at the logs and the chinking, and I think about what life might have been like here almost two hundred years ago. These settlers would have had to learn to live in the woods, to hunt and trap and fish, to trade with the native people who lived in this area. They would have been surrounded by wilderness. Deer would have eaten any attempt at a kitchen garden. Foxes would have killed any chickens.

Sometimes, when you're here, we lie in bed together, making up the particulars of the settlers' days. Up at dawn. No, before that. Wash first. No, light the fire. No, fetch water. The fire wouldn't have been allowed to go out during the night. We can still do it, but just barely, imagine a life that relies entirely on individual labour and effort.

We are playing this game one night when you ask me

about my family, about why I never see them if I live in the same town as they do.

"There's only my father," I say. "My mother died of cancer when I was twelve."

So I tell you the story of my father, of how he worked all his life at the factory, like most of the men in this town. He planed the tables that went into the fancy dining rooms in the houses in the big cities. One of his tables had been bought by Danish royalty. My father liked to imagine royal dinners while we were eating our own vastly inferior version. He was proud that what he had made had gone places he would never go. He told me how at royal dinners guests wiped their hands on dogs at the end of the meal and then the dogs spent all evening licking the grease from their fur.

"I think that happened in medieval times," you say. "Not in twentieth-century dining rooms."

"It was the excess he liked to imagine," I say. "Royalty meant excess to him. Imagine using a wolfhound when a napkin would do. That's the sort of thing he would say."

Those are the happiest memories of my father, those stories. When I was fourteen he cut his hand on a table saw, severed the tendon in his thumb, and damaged the nerves so badly in his wrist that he couldn't use his right hand properly again and lost his job at the factory, had to go on permanent disability.

"And that was the end," I say.

"Of him?"

"No," I say. "Of me."

I can't remember my parents being happy with one another. I don't remember them ever touching, or laughing together, or enjoying any sort of ease. What I remember are isolated moments that didn't seem attached to the story of our life and so never made much sense to me at the time I witnessed them.

One night I got up to go to the bathroom and found my mother sitting in the dry bathtub, in the dark, with her winter coat on.

Several times, when we were having dinner and my mother got up to fetch something, she would walk behind my father's chair and he would flinch as though he expected to be hit.

My parents never talked about how they met. *It's a small town*, my father would say. *We always knew each other*. They never talked about falling in love, and I suspect now that love had little to do with anything in their lives.

Sometimes at the gas station, I will see couples who are happy together. I can recognize it in the easy way they are together, an effortlessness that's evident in their gestures and their words. Nothing is defence or explanation. And I wonder how it's possible that I recognize this happiness, and want it, when I've had so few examples of it in my own life. Is the desire to be loved as instinctual as the need for food and shelter?

On Saturday morning, when the sun is soft through the trees and the dew still sparks on the grass, we begin our search for Lily Steadman.

You pick Malcolm and me up and we drive out to the fields behind Cooper's farm. You have brought your wolf-tracking equipment with you, and the idea is that you and I will go into the woods and Malcolm will stay in the field and track our signal. The woods are vast. They stretch miles from here and we don't want to get lost in our search for Lily.

In order to familiarize Malcolm with the equipment, you ask me to take the wolf collar and enter the woods and walk in one direction, just out of sight of you. The radio frequency is turned on and the antenna picks up my signal as I move among the trees. I can hear you giving instructions to Malcolm to hold the antenna overhead. Inside the woods the air is cool and I walk through shadow. The collar is bulky and I turn it over in my hands, examine the tiny box that holds the radio transmitter. I wonder what the wolves think when they wake from their drugged sleep to find one of these around their necks. They must notice it. It must bother them. You have told me that wolves can range hundreds of miles, so I suppose it would be hopeless to track them without collaring them first. I loop the collar around my own neck. It feels stiff and scratchy and heavier than I'd thought.

When you call me out of the woods I am a good half mile down the treeline, and as I walk back across the field I see that although I left two of you behind, there are now three people waiting for me.

"I thought I'd come out and help Malcolm," says Walter Pendleton.

Malcolm is holding the antenna overhead with his left hand. A bag is slung over his right shoulder that contains the radio. He struts around in front of me.

"I don't really need any help," he says.

"If they get lost," says Walter, "someone will have to drive into town and fetch the police. We've already lost one person."

"This is a precaution," you say sharply, "not a certainty. We're not going to get lost."

Malcolm turns the dial on the radio and the pulse of the signal leaps out into sound.

"Jesus, Malcolm." I wave the collar at him. "I'm right here."

"Just testing," he says.

You take the collar from me and put it in your backpack along with the compass, water, whistle, and food.

"Do you really know what you're doing?" you ask Malcolm. It is an act of faith to leave your research equipment in the hands of such a loony. I wouldn't do it. But you have had less exposure to Malcolm, so perhaps you are able to trust him more.

"Of course," says Malcolm. He waves the antenna around and knocks Walter on the side of the head.

The woods are dense at first, full of brush tangle and seedlings, and we must walk single file. I follow your white shirt and the forest crackles with our footfall. The air swarms with deerflies, held inside the foggy sack of our expelled breath.

We have told ourselves, and each other, that we are here for Lily, but we are also interested in finding the dogs. I had been lying awake last night thinking, not of Lily, but of Hawk. Would she still remember me? Would there still be anything between us? And now, despite the warnings, it seems crazy that we haven't done this before, that we always expected the dogs to come out of the woods to where we were waiting, instead of going into the woods to find them. Never mind all the stories about the ferocious pack of wild dogs. This morning, with the pattern of sun through the trees, with the white flag of your shirt fluttering up ahead of me, our journey towards the dogs seems inevitable, and I'm not afraid.

You are a faster walker than I am, more used to being in the woods, more adept at twisting through the trees, and I often lose you. I can hear you, and can see the flash of your white shirt, like the tail of a deer, bobbing up and down through the trees in front of me. I have to call out to make you stop and wait for me. You don't consider me. I've noticed this before. If I am keeping up with you, am with you, then fine, but if I lag behind, you make no concession for this, just keep on regardless.

Because there seems to be no path through the woods, we can find no evidence of the pack. We don't know what route the dogs travel, and it is unlikely that we are following their trail. The only thing we do find is some very old scat. It is grey and dried out, and when you poke it apart with a stick we can see that it contains mostly hair and teeth.

"Rabbit," you say. We are crouched down on the forest floor. The light pools by your boots.

"Hawk has never caught anything," I say, discouraged at the sight of the badly digested rabbit.

"She didn't need to before," you say. "She will have adapted to meet her new circumstances."

You toss the stick aside, wipe your hands on your jeans, and stand up. You are at ease here, I can see that. You don't need to adapt. You don't have that look I'm used to, that look I thought *was* you, but now I realize could merely be you *with me*. It's a look of apprehension, as though you always have to be wary, as though you are always in danger of being cornered. This is the opposite of what I intend for you and it makes me unbelievably sad to think that you can feel trapped by me.

"I love you," I say, and I put my hand on the back of your shirt, warm from the sun. I am always touching you. I can't help myself.

"I love you too," you say, and you take my hand and we move farther into the woods.

We call out to Lily. We call out to Hawk, and to Lopez, and to Jamie's dog, Scout. We use the whistle and the high, shrill bridge of sound reaches out to connect where we are with where we are headed.

There is no answer to any of our efforts. After a couple of hours we stop, drink some water, eat an apple. You lean against a tree and I lean against you, and we don't say anything. The light funnels down from above, slops onto the patch of ground by our feet.

At the edge of the woods, where we usually wait, the trees are mostly coniferous—pine and spruce and hemlock. Farther into the woods there are other kinds of trees—maples, birches, the smooth-barked beech. Farther into the woods everything isn't so tangled up with itself. There are small clearings, and areas of hummocky ground where fallen, rotten trees make up the forest floor.

I have never been this far into the woods and it amazes me that I haven't. It must have been fear that kept me to the edges, to the safe places—fear and the idea that what was deep in the woods would be no different from what was on the perimeter. But this is not true. Each square inch of ground holds different secrets. Deep in the woods one is held by the surrounding wilderness. Here we are at the centre of things. Here we are the fire in this green furnace.

We don't find the dogs or Lily. We never discover any other evidence to suggest that the dogs are even in here, and we find nothing to tell us that Lily might also be here. And in the end, after we have spent much of the day tromping through the bush, getting scratched by branches and constantly losing our way, and we are tired and hungry, we tell ourselves that it's good the dogs are well hidden, that this will keep them safe. We tell ourselves that it is impossible that Lily Steadman could have gone after them into these woods.

Later that night I take you with me to spy on Malcolm. On the nights when you stay over, Malcolm doesn't come to the cabin after dinner to chat. His absence, on the nights you are with me, makes me realize that he is probably spying on me as certainly as I am spying on him.

It's almost midnight when we creep through the woods to the farmhouse, but all the lights are on when we get there. Your years spent observing animals in the wild have made you a very good spy and I walk along quietly behind you as you stealthily move along the perimeter of the building. I rise as you rise to peer into each lit square of window.

Malcolm is in the living room. He is painting. He has an easel set up behind the couch and a canvas set upon the easel. When we look through the window we see the back of the easel and his eyes staring at the canvas. We can't see what he is painting. The moment resolved, I think, remembering our earlier conversation. But what moment is it? We watch for a while and then creep back through the woods to the cabin.

"You could come and stay with me," you say. "If you're nervous about being here."

"But I'm not nervous," I say. I'm not really afraid of Malcolm, even if I should be. He never seems to actually want to come into my cabin, and I have grown used to our strange after-dinner conversations on the steps. As much as I love you, I don't want to stay with you in your borrowed apartment in town. Nothing in that place reminds me of you and I'm disturbed by that. "He's only painting," I say.

"Still . . ." you say, but you don't finish the thought. When we're lying in bed later, you say, "I don't want anything to happen to you." And when we have sex I can feel an anxiety in your body that hasn't been there before.

I used to think that sex was about being in the present, existing entirely in the moment, and I was always grateful for the relief of that. But sex with you is different. Even though we don't talk too much about the details, I think we've both had hard lives, and we've settled for things we shouldn't have settled for, and at the heart of both of us is a mix of grief, anger, and loneliness. Sex with you feels like a push to get back to an uncorrupted, unviolated self, and I sometimes feel bits of my old life float up to the surface and time becomes confused and it seems as though you've always been here, always been with me. I am returned to a self that I wasn't aware I'd ever lost so absolutely.

What swims back to me when I'm lying under you? The sensation I used to have on the motorcycle when I'd been riding for too long—a feeling as though I could just step off onto the air beside the bike and it would hold me up; the lean of the wind against my chest, and my surrender to it. Or the stumble of my body as I ran beside the river as a child, looking for the right place to hurl myself off the bank into the ashen boil of the current. The flex of my breath against my ribs and the rush of the water under my outstretched arms. The fear that I wouldn't make it across to the other side. The fierce hope that I would.

I lie awake this night, after you have fallen off to sleep, after the wind has rattled the windows of the cabin, and the owl has sung its hunting song. I lie awake and I think of these moments of myself that come back to me through you. The moment resolved, that is what it is sometimes, to be with you. The moment of myself, revisited and redeemed.

On Sunday evening we debate about going to the police and telling them that Lily Steadman does not have a boyfriend, that she used to come out every evening to the woods and wait with us for the dogs to return. Just as we all decide that we'd better divulge what we know, even though our own behaviour will come under scrutiny, the police drop the whole boyfriend tangent. Walter arrives to tell us they have investigated and found out that there is no boyfriend. And, more importantly, there's been a sighting of Lily Steadman wandering along the tracks by the old railway station.

*   *   *

You take me up to where the wolves are. You want to go and check on the pack and you ask me to go with you. We drive north for hours, hike through the forest, and make camp on the edge of a lake.

At night we lie awake, listening for the wolves to howl. The moon outside the tent makes a strange green glow through the trees. There is the noise of twigs snapping and the scuffing of small animals in the dirt. I have never heard wolves howl and I fall asleep still listening, wake to something I can't quite place, something that doesn't sound the way I think it should, but which I realize suddenly *is* the sound of wolves howling. I whisper your name, but you're already awake, and we lie there, in the tent, listening. They sound nearby. I had expected a chorus of howls, all the voices raised together, but the sound is quite different from that. One wolf howls, long notes of descant, and underneath, supporting the notes, are the barks and yips of other wolves. It is as if they are encouraging the main howler, urging him on, that the howl, instead of being something done in unison, is more like polyphony. Each voice is audible, each voice can be distinguished from the others, each voice can be followed as a separate thread, and yet the music that they make together is no less together because of that.

The howls fill the night around the tent, the space around us, and I am glad, no, honoured, that I have heard this unimaginable sound with you.

The next morning you decide to go into the woods and look for the wolves. The howls last night have encouraged you that the wolves are perhaps close enough to track. I want to go with you, but you make a case for going alone, saying it's work and you will be able to make faster progress without me. You are distant this morning, efficiently rounding up your gear, striding off through the trees with a wave of your hand. You were impatient with me when I tried to help you get ready, accused me of fussing, brushed aside the package of food I had prepared for you. So it is a relief, really, when you go, and I am left to read by the edge of the lake in the slow, returning sun.

Because I am still, sitting on the rocks warmed by the sun at the edge of the water, the animals whose world this is start to show themselves to me. I stop reading and watch them, as I imagine you watch the wolves, trying to determine truths from their observed patterns of behaviour.

Heron: No fish from the long attentive stillness on the rock. No fish from creeping down the slanted log, to stand in the shallows by the sunning turtles. It doesn't work to imitate a stick, to stretch the neck to heaven and become thin as a whisper. There is sometimes no reward for patience. If hunger is the engine, life is only either underway or stalled; and desire is just a watered-down version of hunger, a poor copy. Desire is what I have as the watcher, wanting there to be fish at one of the stations of the heron, wanting the story to go the way it should, for effort to be rewarded, for a hunger most people can no longer feel in themselves to be satisfied in this elegant, feathered creature of will.

Fish: Late afternoon they swim to the shallow water off the rock, hang in the warmth of the sun, and flick flies from the surface. Motionless, they make a wheel, heads to the outside, tails to the centre. Any danger will be instantly spotted and they can all flash off in the opposite direction. But what the fish can't see is the osprey circling above them, drawing his own lazy wheel of hunger over the water. When he dives suddenly and plucks a fish from its soft room, I know this—every creature does the best it can to defend its life. Death waits just beyond the danger we can imagine.

Woodpecker: The pileated woodpecker has sawdust on her head as she hammers her hunger into the rotten birch tree by the water. She is not disturbed by human sounds, other birds, or planes. She flies off with a loud cry at dusk and I imagine she returns uttering the same cry at dawn. Sometimes she jams her entire head into the hole she has made, following the thin trickle of termites up the blind river of their own hunger.

Duck: The merganser swoops up from the lake and then swoops back down, always landing in exactly the same place. What seems to matter is the announcement of territory. The flights are short and swift, do not yield any food, are not taken with any companions. If one is made for air and water, is this truth to be constantly proved? Does the memory of floating and flying swing the body up and then float the body down?

Fish: The dead fish drift down the lake, float into the bay near to where I am sitting. What killed them? Do they have a nest of fish hooks in their guts? Is the lake itself poison now? Whatever the cause, the fish bump against the weeds massed at the edge of the swamp. A milky eye to heaven. A milky eye to the dark water. The frogs start the small engine of their breath at dusk, and something starts eating the dead fish from the water side. When they are flipped over, pink flesh, entrails that unravel in the weeds. They are being consumed by the world they inhabited. And in the world they visit—that flat, blank sky above them—they float undisturbed. The fish never had a desire to be here, and this world has no desire to taste them now.

Raccoon: The raccoon, frightened up the tree by a noise from me, stutters a soft grunt, like a motor that can't get started. When he finally swings out of the branches, he comes down the tree headfirst, awkward and slow, stopping to sniff the air on the way down. The dead fish he has followed the shoreline to claim lies near the water at the base of the tree. The raccoon rips the skin back and chews on the flesh beneath. He eats open-mouthed, like a dog. The flesh of the fish is white and viscous, oily with decay. And just as it seems he's enjoying his meal, the raccoon stops eating, lays the fish at the base of the tree, and scrambles away into the woods. There was no danger. No other animals approached him. There was no sound from me. He hadn't eaten enough to be full.

Hunger is a beginning I can understand. It is most beginnings. But it is in endings that we prove our aloneness, and our individuality. To give up on, in an instant, what we worked so hard to get is what we have to fear from one another.

You don't get back until after dark. I'm already in the tent when I hear you scraping around outside, looking for food. At first I think an animal has wandered into the camp, but then I hear you swear as you struggle with the bear rope, as you try to release the food pack from its perch slung up high over a branch in the pine tree. When I come out of the tent you're clattering around inside the plastic food barrel.

"Sorry," you say. "I didn't mean to wake you."

"I wasn't asleep." I take the flashlight from your hand, shine it into the barrel, and retrieve the package of food I'd made for you earlier. "Here." I pass it over.

We sit on the log by the firepit. I didn't bother to make a fire, not wanting to sit there, waiting for you all evening, and the heap of cold ash looks milky in the pass of moonlight coming through the trees. It's cold. I pull the sleeves of my sweatshirt down over my hands.

"Did you find them?" I ask.

I am angry at you for leaving me, angry at you for taking so long to come back. You have your mouth full of sandwich, don't answer me right away.

"Did you find your wolves?" I ask again.

"No. They weren't where I thought they'd be, where they'd been before. They sounded close last night, but they weren't close."

You sound angry too. You sound as though you're angry with me, as though you blame me for your not being able to track the wolves down.

"Maybe they were close last night," I say. "And then they moved off." I refuse to carry the responsibility of your disappointment.

You brush your hands firmly against your pant legs, crumple the foil I had wrapped your food in, and toss it into the firepit. "Exactly," you say, and you get up and go into the tent.

Nothing is the same between us after this night. You pull away from me. You find excuses not to see me. Traits in me that you had previously found appealing you now find intolerable. I can't figure it out. All I can think is that you haven't been honest with me, that you weren't feeling what you said you were feeling, that you weren't really in love with me. This explanation makes sense, or the opposite, that you are more controlled by fear than I'd realized, that it felt terrible to you to be open with another person and you couldn't sustain it;

you had to shut down, turn away. Both of these things are painful to face and there is no way I can hope to win against them. The love I have for you is not going to be stronger than either your fear or your indifference. I have no chance.

After you go into the tent, that night by the lake, I sit out by the cold fire. When the moon comes out from behind a cloud the crumpled tinfoil in the firepit flickers silver and then goes out. I sit out there until I am too cold to bear it any longer and then I hang the food barrel back up in the tree and go into the tent where you sleep. All night long I lie beside you and listen to your breathing. All night long I lie beside you, listening for the wolves to howl, but I never hear them again.

When we return to town you drop me off at the cabin and then I don't hear from you for three days. In that time Malcolm reappears on my porch steps after supper. I know I must be missing you dreadfully because I am positively joyful at seeing him the first evening, bound out of the cabin when I hear the first tentative creak of his footsteps on the rotted wooden boards.

Malcolm has black paint on his fingernails and white paint in his hair. There's a smear of green on the grubby T-shirt he wears.

"You've been painting," I say.

"I've been painting." He drops down on the steps and pushes his feet out in front of him. I drop down beside him.

"What have you been painting?" I ask.

"I can't tell you that," he says, "until it's finished. If I tell you now, it might change into something else."

"Why would it do that?"

"It just might," he says, looking right and left suspiciously as though someone is lurking around the cabin, listening to his every word.

If you don't return and I'm left with only Malcolm for company, I will go crazy. It's bad enough that we don't go and wait for the dogs any more, that the expectation of seeing them again has evaporated, but if my only social outing is sitting on the steps with Malcolm after dinner and being glad of it, I might as well pack up and leave town.

"What does your mother think of your painting?" I ask Malcolm.

"My mother?" He looks stricken, and because I'm missing you so badly and don't really care about anything else at the moment, I decide to ask him what I've wanted to know since I arrived here.

"Your mother doesn't exist," I say, "does she? I've never seen her about. You never go anywhere with her." I stare at Malcolm and he stares back at me with panic in his eyes. "Come on," I say impatiently. "Just tell me the truth. Does she exist or not?"

"She used to exist," he says. "But she doesn't any more."

"Where is she, then?"

"Dead." Malcolm pulls his knees in and wraps his arms around them. "She's been dead for years now."

"But you said she'd had a stroke. You said you had to move here to look after her."

Malcolm grins at me, a big, goofy, insane sort of grin. "I didn't think you'd move into the cabin if you knew I lived out here alone."

"And why did you want me to move into the cabin?"

"I just did." Malcolm puts his forehead down on his arms and says something I can't hear through his knees.

"What?"

"She was a crazy lady," he says, still muffled, but audible. "My mother. She was one crazy lady."

That night, after Malcolm has scurried off, I lie in the bed in the cabin, and for the first time I'm afraid. I don't know when I'm to see you again. I don't know what goes on in Malcolm's head and what he intends for me. I don't trust him, and I don't know him at all. It's time to leave this place. Tomorrow I will start looking through the want ads for something to rent.

I'm working nights this week, and every afternoon, before I head over to the gas station, I drive past your apartment, hoping to catch a glimpse of you. But your truck isn't there and tonight I drive to work disappointed and anxious, stopping to get a paper on the way so that I can look for an apartment while I'm waiting out my shift in the booth.

Nights are better to work than days at the gas station. They are quieter. There's a bulge of activity around suppertime, when people are coming home from work, and another burst of traffic in the early evening, as people head out to their various activities, but between nine o'clock and eleven it's pretty dead. I prefer working nights to days. I can read or listen to the radio when there are no customers.

This shift goes fairly smoothly at the beginning. The flow of cars is steady until about nine o'clock and then it eases off. I spread the newspaper out on the desk and start looking through the listings of apartments for rent. I can't afford much, with the wages I make at the gas station, and there is not much on offer anyway.

Outside the booth the asphalt looks wet under the street lights and the cars hum along the wire of highway. I had expected better things from my life than what has happened. I was meant to be making a home with John and going to school. Instead I am painfully in love with you and living in a cabin in the woods that belongs to someone who might possibly murder me. I'm working at the sort of job I should have left behind long ago. I've even lost my dog, perhaps the creature who loved me best on this earth.

I close the newspaper and lean back in the chair. The

inside of the booth smells oily and rancid. The lights on the highway flash and disappear, like a word that flares into speech and then is gone; like all the words you ever said to me. The sweetest things anyone has ever said to me; possibly all lies.

A car pulls into the gas station, not up to the pumps but right up against the booth. It's most likely people who need directions, or want to borrow a gas can. I watch, unalarmed, as four teenage boys spill out of the car. Even when they jam themselves inside the booth, I don't think anything of it. But then I see that one of the boys has a gun and that one of the boys is Jamie.

We stare at one another across the plastic counter pouched with lottery tickets. He seems just as astonished to see me as I am to see him. The boy with the gun waves it at me.

"Give me the money, bitch," he says.

The boys are jumped up with the excitement of what they are doing. They jostle together in the small space of the booth, like cattle being herded into a pen. The windows steam up with their fevered breath. Someone knocks over the stand with the maps on it.

I have been robbed before, when I was younger and working at another gas station. I know that the best thing to do is to stay calm and give them what they want. I open the till. The boy with the gun flaps it in my face. The tip of the barrel grazes my nose and I try not to flinch.

"This is all there is," I say, scooping the bills from the drawer of the register. I have just made a deposit in the safe, through its metal flap. It is customary to skim two hundred dollars off the cash float whenever it mounts up.

"Where's the safe?" says the boy with the gun. I point to the metal cube under the counter and he launches himself onto my side of the booth, kicks at the safe with his running shoe.

"It's bolted to the floor," I say. "And I don't have the

combination." My hand still holds the ruff of bills I've lifted from the cash drawer.

The boy with the gun kicks at the safe again. "Who has the combination?" he says.

"The manager."

"Call him."

I look at Jamie, who's looking in panic at me. "What am I supposed to say?"

"Let's just take the money and go," says Jamie.

The boy with the gun presses it against my forehead.

"Fuck," says Jamie. "Don't do that."

"Call him," says the boy with the gun, and I put the money down on the counter and reach my shaking hand towards the phone. The boy with the gun is sweating. I can see the moisture on his upper lip and forehead. I am afraid now and the boys know it. They become more boisterous, knocking against one another in clumsy excitement. Someone has stinky feet. The acrid tang of foot odour fills the confines of the booth.

Sometimes in my life I have considered dying and I have felt that it might be a relief not to have to continue with the excruciating pain of existence. But whenever I have thought about dying, it has been about ending my life myself. I do not want to be shot by a boy who hasn't even made it through puberty yet.

The manager of the gas station is a woman, not a man, but I don't want to correct the boy with the gun in case it makes him angrier. He already seems well ignited by his rage and fear. The manager's name is Darlene, and because she has small children it's a safe bet that she'll be home late at night. I punch her number into the phone and wait for the ring.

"Shit," says one of the boys, and just as the phone rings in Darlene's townhouse, I see the swirling lights of the police car.

The phone is knocked from my hand and the boy with

the gun swings at my head, but I move far enough out of reach so that he merely grazes my cheek with the barrel of the gun.

The boys lunge at the door and I follow them out.

"Jamie," I say. He is last to exit the booth, closest to me. The other boys are at their car. They open the doors. Jamie stands on the piece of asphalt between the car and me. "Come here," I say, and he does. I pull him down quickly behind the oil display just as the car with the boys in it squeals out of the parking lot and the police car squeals after it, lights on, siren open.

Someone must have either pulled in for gas or seen what was happening from the road and called the police. I have no doubt the boys will be caught. They don't seem old enough to drive, let alone to have figured out any sort of contingency plan.

Jamie squats beside me behind the plastic stand of oil bottles. He is sweating through his T-shirt, and his breathing is short and shallow. I put my arm around him, and though at first he flinches away, he then leans clumsily against me, like a big dog trying to fit onto a small lap.

"They'll be caught," I say. "We have to get you away from here."

"Alice," he says, and his voice sounds shaky with nerves or the effort to keep from crying. "I didn't know you worked here."

"It's okay." I haul him to his feet and pull him across the parking lot to my car. There's no one around to see us, and if we can get out of here fast enough, I might be able to make this work. I was scared, I will say, later. I just took off in a panic. No, I never saw a fourth boy. He must have run out across the highway.

Jamie is crying by the time we're in the car and heading out of the parking lot, away from the gas station. He puts his hands up to his face and leans against the side window.

He sobs as though he's drowning, and it takes a while before he can push any words out.

"They'll kill me," he says, and I don't know whether he means his parents or the boys in the car.

"I'm taking you to the cabin," I say. "Don't worry." For I am glad to see Jamie again and I am unwilling to surrender him for now.

At the cabin everything feels better, more in control. I light the lamps and sit Jamie down at the table.

"Do you want anything to eat?" I ask. I have turned the stove on and am making myself a cup of tea.

Jamie shakes his head, no.

"Have you done that before?" I ask, placing the kettle on the burner and dropping a tea bag into my mug.

"Not that."

"What, then?"

"Other things." Jamie shrugs his shoulders. "I never hurt anybody," he says. "I wouldn't do that."

"I know." I make the tea and sit down opposite him at the table. Outside I can hear the crickets stretch their net of music across the dark.

I'll have to quit that stupid job, I think, and I am relieved at the thought.

"What do you want to do?" I ask Jamie.

"Stay here."

"You can't stay here forever. Your parents will be looking for you."

Jamie wraps his arms around his chest. He looks both defiant and afraid, a look I remember from my own younger self. "I don't want to go to jail," he says.

"That won't happen." The robbery didn't even work. The money wasn't taken. All the boys really did was knock over the map rack and wave the gun around and stink up the booth with their body odour. "You'll probably get some community service and a record until you're eighteen."

"How do you know?" Jamie regards me suspiciously.

"Because that's how it was for me and my friends when I was your age. I'm sure the system hasn't changed that much since then."

"What did you do?"

"Stole a car, drank underage. There was one case of arson that couldn't be proved and one case that could."

"Cool." Jamie looks at me with new respect.

"Not really," I say. "Look at how I've ended up."

"You haven't ended," says Jamie.

We look at one another over the table. I miss you. I don't know what I'll do if you don't come back. "Haven't I?" I say, for I can't imagine anything more for myself, anything that isn't this moment, or a continuation of all the other fucked-up moments of my life.

"No," says Jamie, with certainty. "You are nowhere near ended."

At that moment there's a sort of squeal and the cabin door flies open and Malcolm stands in the doorway holding what looks to be a speargun.

"I won't let you do it," he says, advancing quickly into the interior of the cabin.

Jamie and I both jump up from the table and I see that what Malcolm thrusts alarmingly before him *is* a speargun.

"What the fuck," says Jamie, "are you doing?" He has come over to my side of the table and we are both pressed up against the cabin wall.

Malcolm pushes the tip of the speargun between us and tries to lever Jamie away from me. "Run, run," he says urgently. "I'll stop her. I'll save you."

"What are you talking about?" says Jamie.

"What are you doing?" I say.

"You don't need to be a prisoner," says Malcolm.

"What prisoner?" says Jamie.

And while Malcolm is addressing Jamie I put my hand on the rusted tip of the speargun and gently start to steer it towards the floor.

"You don't need that," I say.

"Don't I?" says Malcolm. He looks confused.

"No." I push the tip of the speargun all the way to the floor and squeeze out from behind the table. "What do you need?" I say.

"Need?"

"Yes."

Malcolm drops the speargun on the floor. It clatters hard against the wood and then there is only the noise of him breathing and outside the sound of the crickets still. "I went off the pills so I could paint," he says.

"Never a good idea," mutters Jamie from behind me.

Malcolm goes over to the bed and sits down so heavily on it that it moves a little way across the floor. His face is grey and there's sweat on his forehead. He is blinking more than seems normal. He appears defeated, and when I look at him I can see how he will age, how parts of him will become more pronounced and parts will sink away, like something turning slowly in the water, revealing itself and submerging itself with every movement.

"I'm sorry," says Malcolm. He puts his head in his hands and begins to cry quietly.

Jamie is kneeling on the floor looking at the speargun. "Is this for underwater?" he asks. "Could I catch a whale with it?"

Malcolm starts to rock back and forth. The bed squeaks and moves a few inches every time he leans forward, every time he leans back. It sounds like the crickets outside. The bigger noise and the smaller noise overlap and disappear into each other.

We take Malcolm back to the farmhouse. He is calmer there, sits in a tatty armchair in the living room and lets me make him a cup of tea. Jamie is fascinated with the mess of the place, wanders from room to room, returning every so often to show me an object of wonder. An old hand grenade. A potato so dried out it seems like a knotted piece of wood. A necklace of shark's teeth.

I pull up a chair beside Malcolm. "Can I call someone for you?" I ask.

Malcolm shakes his head. "There's no one," he says.

I don't call anyone for Malcolm, but I do call my manager, Darlene, and explain that I panicked and that I haven't been kidnapped or shot, but she's very unsympathetic.

"The police called. You left the money out on the counter," she says. "In broad daylight."

"It was dark," I say. "Night, not daylight." The phone in Malcolm's house is balanced on a huge stack of advertising flyers from at least ten years ago. I don't remember ground beef ever being that cheap.

"It's just an expression, Alice," says Darlene. She sounds exasperated with me. I had been expecting a little more concern for my safety. In the background I can hear the laugh track of some comedy show on her TV. She hasn't even turned it down to speak to me.

"I'm going to have to quit, Darlene," I say.

"Well, I would have had to fire you anyways," she says, and with that we both end our entirely unsatisfactory conversation.

Jamie comes for me as I hang up the phone. "You have to

see this," he says, and he leads me into one of the small rooms off the kitchen. There, stacked against a wall, are Malcolm's paintings.

"Look." Jamie flicks each painting forward so I can see what he has discovered. Each one of the canvases has been painted utterly black.

I send Jamie back to the cabin and I wait with Malcolm until he seems calm enough to leave. I sit opposite him, both of us drinking our tea and watching one another. Malcolm has the watery, rather desperate eyes of a man who has given up something powerful but hasn't replaced it with anything else that is as satisfying, anything else that requires the kind of commitment that serious addiction demands.

"You're kind," says Malcolm.

Kind is the last thing I really feel. It's awkward because I am obligated to him for letting me stay in the cabin, and now that I've got Jamie in there as well, at least temporarily, I feel even more obliged towards Malcolm.

"It's the least I can do," I say. I want to say that it's the most I will do, but I sip my tea and tell myself to be grateful that I've had a place to stay this month.

"You're kind and beautiful," says Malcolm, and then I understand. In his crazy, inarticulate way, Malcolm Dodd is in love with me. Suddenly his bizarre behaviour makes more sense. Madness driven by love I do understand. But I don't want to enter into a conversation about his feelings for me, and after our tea is finished and I've offered again to call someone for Malcolm and he's again declined, I make my way back through the woods to the cabin.

Jamie is sitting at the table trying to take the hand grenade apart with a paring knife.

"You would have exploded by now if that thing had any sort of charge left in it, right?"

"Right," says Jamie, not looking up. "Did you have him taken away?"

"I can't do that."

"You should do that."

"He's obviously got some problems."

"Obviously." Jamie pries the outer casing off the hand grenade and lays it carefully on the table. "As long as he won't be back here again tonight."

"Hopefully not." I don't think I can handle any more excitement. I'll have to quit this cabin as I quit my job. And then there's the problem of Jamie. I look at him, cheerfully absorbed in his dissection of the hand grenade, and I have no idea what to do about him.

"I'm going to make you a bed on the floor," I say, dragging some of the blankets off my bed and searching around for something to use as a pillow.

"Okay," says Jamie.

"It might not be that comfortable."

"That's fine."

When we've taken our separate trips to the outhouse and I've made Jamie wash his hands in a bowl of water from the stream and I've brushed my teeth and given him toothpaste to smear over his and the lamps have been blown out and we've crawled into our respective beds with most of our clothes still on, he calls out to me across the few feet of worn and silent dark.

"Alice?"

"What?"

"Thank you for keeping me."

I don't know what to say, because I can't be keeping him. Even if the trouble had never happened tonight, Jamie belongs elsewhere, and in the morning all of that will have to be faced. But for now he is here, and I know he is safe with me. No harm will come to him, and that makes me feel good.

"Go to sleep," I say.

I hear the engine before I'm properly awake, lying in the early morning chill of the cabin, listening to Jamie making snuffling noises on the floor beside my bed. I haven't opened my eyes yet, lie on my back in the darkness that, moments ago, was the room of my dream and is now the room of my waking.

The engine makes a heavy, rhythmic knocking, as if a knotted rope is being flung about under the hood of the truck. Your truck. I sit up and open my eyes. I am out of the cabin before you're out of the truck, and even though I know that my love for you makes me weak and foolish, I cannot stop my joy at seeing you again. It is as though my body has been lifted up by the sight of you stepping out of the truck cab. I don't feel the ground under my feet, all I do is cover the distance between my body and yours—everything else is just getting there.

I throw myself at you as you step away from the truck, step towards me, and I feel two things in that moment. I feel the impossible relief that spills from my body at the certain feel of your skin, and I feel the undeniable instant of your stiffening under my embrace.

"Alice," you say, and you hold me at arm's length, away from you. "They've sent hunters into the woods after the dogs."

For weeks now we have heard the rumblings about the damage the wild dogs have been doing to the livestock on the various farms in the area, and we have ignored them. There was an article last week in the local paper showing a photograph of a sheep that had been ripped to pieces by the dogs. Its skin had been neatly peeled back on one side, like a carpet stripped back to reveal a coveted piece of hardwood flooring.

"We have to go," you say. "We might be too late, but we have to try and stop it."

I run around the front of the truck to climb into the cab on the passenger side. The engine ticks slowly down like a metronome and the metal of the hood is warm where it brushes against my arm. I stop with my hand on the edge of the door.

"Jamie's here," I say.

"Well, he can't come with us."

"He can't stay here." I don't know what state Malcolm will wake up in this morning. "Just wait a minute," I say, and I run back to the cabin.

Jamie is still burrowed into his nest of blankets on the floor. I bend down and shake him awake. "Get up," I say. "We have to go. They're going to shoot the dogs."

Jamie sits between us in the truck and I can tell you're glad of that. His hair is still tangled from sleep and his shoelaces are untied. He yawns and doesn't cover his mouth, rubs his eyes hard as we lurch out of the driveway onto the road. None of us speaks on the way to the woods. You drive with a fierce concentration, arms braced rigid against the steering wheel. Houses flash by, like clothes pinned out on the line of highway, each one a square of white or a triangle of blue, here and gone in an instant.

We park where we used to park when we'd gather in the evenings to wait for the dogs, out behind the fields on Cooper's farm. The truck is barely stopped before we all burst out of the cab. But we're too late. The men have already emerged from the woods. We can see them approaching from across the field. They walk in a single line, swaying out and back, like the tail of an animal flicking behind the body.

"They're carrying things," says Jamie. He rubs his eyes, still sleepy.

I look at you and you look at me and I know we are

thinking the same thing. I put my hand on Jamie's shoulder and he flinches.

"What?" he says. But by this time the men have moved that much closer and he understands.

The men walk in single file. One of them wears a dead dog, draped around his neck like a fur ruff. The dog's head bobs up and down rather tenderly against his shoulder, like a sleeping child. There's blood on the fur and the wind lifts the loose tendrils on the flanks that aren't matted down with that same blood.

"That's Lopez," you say.

"There's my dog," says Jamie. "There's Scout."

We stand by the truck at the edge of the woods as the hunters come out from the trees with the bodies. The men are grim-faced. Their lips are set in hard lines and they funnel their gaze purposefully ahead. They do not look at us as they pass.

Lily is in the arms of the last man. She is still wearing the cardigan she always had on, but it is so embedded with dirt that it looks to be brown and not pink. Her hair is matted over her face, stuck to her skin with her own blood. She has been shot in the head. One of her ears has come unstuck from its moorings, flaps against the side of her skull as the man who carries her steps forward over the uneven ground. And all over her body are leaves, pasted onto her clothes and skin. As she is carried past us, they unpeel from her, drift slowly down on the thin current of air her dead body displaces, air that is made from the breath of the hunters. The leaves swirl around us as she passes, each one perfect and over, each one a prayer we couldn't speak, wafting down to clothe us.

I know now that you will leave me. I know that I will always love you. I know that I cannot be saved, and neither can Jamie, and neither can you. We will go on, alone, into a space we once defined together. I know that the world in which we existed will not remember us at all. I know that *this* can never be *that*, that faith isn't belief but struggle with belief.

I know too that we could have saved the dogs and Lily. Our mistake was in believing that they were more attached to us than we were to them, that they would come out of the woods, that their memory of what they'd had with us would be more powerful than their new life without us. We couldn't imagine a world for them where we weren't central.

I love you. It rises up in me sure as breath, but what I cannot escape is the fact that you didn't want what I could give you. You left. What you didn't want was me, and I feel fooled into believing something existed where obviously nothing ever did.

And when I think of you now I think of the woodthrush that flew into the cabin window one day that summer; how I picked its still body up from the porch and held it in my hands. It lay there for a few moments, stunned, and then it flickered back and clambered up on my finger, looking around at a world changed and still recognizable. I tried to encourage it to fly off, but the bird wouldn't leave my finger. I walked around the porch and down onto the forest floor, and still it wouldn't leave. I even went inside the cabin and it stayed clipped to my index finger with its scaly, hooked feet. A woodthrush is a pretty bird. I stroked its throat and looked into its wet, dark eyes. I spoke to it. And just when I became convinced that the bird had somehow formed an attachment to me, that it had chosen to stay with me, that I was blessed with its wild trust—it flew off. It had been more dazed than I'd realized from flying into the window and it had merely taken a long time to recover its senses.

*   *   *

This is the prayer I cannot speak to you, but it is yours
nonetheless:

I lay down in the tall meadow grasses.
I lay down in the fragrant song of earth.
I lay down in the polish of the morning and the
    tarnish of the evening.
I lay down in rain.
I lay down under the word as promise and the word
    as deed.
I lay down alone.
I lay down in the hollows made by ice and rock and
    filled each year with winter.
I lay down on the hard stone bed of grief.
I lay down with the taste of sunlight on my skin, with
    summer in my mouth, with a veil of bees around
    my hair.
I lay down with dying in my bones.
I lay down under the sweet, anxious sorrow of you.

I rise up from water, from air, from the hard body of
    the earth.
I rise up into memory, into springtime, into all I once
    held by name.
I rise up with hope for the new day.
I rise up in mourning.
I rise up with the taste of loss bitter on my tongue and
    your name still warm on my skin.
I rise up from the soft, dark room of sleep, blank as
    water.
I rise up with the whispered secrets of the insects a
    woven lace above my eyes.
I rise up.
(Say it.)
I rise up from your body for the last time.

two

jamie

It's fifteen steps from the back door to the fridge. If I pull the fridge door back against the hinge, it will open without a sound. The bread wrapper will crinkle. Yogurt makes that suction scoop when you pull the foil top off. The cheese drawer sticks on its runners. Peanut butter will be all right. I can twist the plastic cap off slowly and it won't make any noise. I can stand here at the fridge and shove my fingers into the jar instead of risking the rustle of the cutlery drawer.

It was easier when the dog was here. I didn't go out so much then, but if I was out, he would wait for me by the back door, stand with me here, our noses inside the fridge. Dogs can be very quiet. If I was eating peanut butter, I would smear some of it on the top of his nose and he would spend ages licking it off. I liked to watch him do that.

Alice says the dogs are probably doing fine without us in the woods, but I don't believe her. She says things to protect me, and some days I'm glad of this, but some days it just makes me mad. I'm pretty sure that Alice has had some bad stuff happen in her life and so I don't like her to know that I'm mad at her. People who have had a lot of bad things need a lot of good things to balance everything out, and I know Alice is trying to make good things happen, to live as though good things are happening. But I don't believe this either.

I can't say anything because Alice wouldn't listen to me. She doesn't pay me as much attention as she pays the wolf woman. That's how it is. There's always someone you listen to the most. There's always someone you believe above all others.

I used to be like that with my father. I liked it when he told me things. I liked listening to him. But he's been gone for so long now I can't remember any of that stuff any more. I can't even really remember what he looked like or what his shirt smelled like when he carried me up against his shoulder. And I am so pissed at him for leaving that I wouldn't even be glad to see him if he did come back.

I'm not mad at Scout. It wasn't his fault. He didn't leave on purpose.

The peanut butter lid sticks a little, but I ease it off slowly. The light from the fridge makes a small puddle of brightness by my feet. I wish I could drink it up. I wish I could still feel that feeling I used to have when I was little because it was like that, it was like I'd swallowed light and could glow from the inside.

There's a small squelching noise behind me. I stiffen, my hand frozen above the peanut butter jar, but it's only my mother. She is right behind me, breathes into my ear.

"Hi, baby," she whispers. "You're so late. Would you like me to make you something to eat?"

I shake my head, no. It's a brave thing for her to say because we both know it would make too much noise if she did make me a sandwich or put something in the microwave. She puts a hand briefly, gently, on my back, and it's hard not to shake it off, even though I know it's *her* hand. I don't like to be touched. I sort of flick my shoulder and she takes her hand away.

"I'm okay," I whisper, and I don't even turn around to her. And there is nothing for her to do now but to leave the kitchen. She does this, as silently as she came into it. She moves so easily, not needing to feel her way between the furniture and the walls, that I know she must have counted the steps as well, and knowing this makes me hate her.

It is good to be out of the house as much as possible. Before I stopped going to wait for the dogs I used to hang out with friends, go to someone's house and watch TV or play video games. But something happened after I stopped going to the woods last August. I got bored with my friends. I got bored just sitting around playing games like a child. My body couldn't keep still the way it had once wanted to. I found new friends, older kids who let me hang out with them because I showed them how brave I could be. They were easy to impress, these older guys—break into a few cars, pry the screen off a basement window and crawl inside to steal whatever was lying within reach. I was good at that. I was good at being quiet. I could even sneak through someone's house when the people were still in it, and they wouldn't notice a thing. I felt proud of myself for never once getting caught, for never once hearing someone say, *Who's down there?* and having to throw myself back out the basement window and run like shit across the grass behind the house.

I didn't really care about the stealing. I don't want things, or even money. I liked going down to the old factory along the river, the place where everyone in this town used to work and where no one works now, and I liked to break the windows. There is something, well, beautiful, about the sound of a window breaking. It's final, that's the best word for it, and it sounds exactly like what it is—crackly and high and kind of like a scream that stops and starts again—and when the window breaks, it sounds too like all the other glass noises. There's the happy touch of two glasses, and the watery ripple of chimes, and the clatter of the dog's bowl on the cement of the back steps. And every time I flung my arm back and flung my arm forward, made that swimming motion in the air, and the rock arced up into the night, I got all of that. I got to have all the sounds in one sound, all the things in one movement of my arm. I made something by destroying those windows, and I liked how that felt.

*   *   *

It wasn't that I didn't like those other people who waited by the woods out behind Cooper's farm. It's true I always thought that Malcolm was weird and I didn't trust the wolf woman, but I liked Alice, and I liked Lily. I felt sorry for Lily because she wanted her dog back even more than I wanted Scout to come out from the trees, and at a certain point I knew this wasn't going to happen, and I know, from the way she was, that Lily would never be able to know this. I suppose I was fooled by the dogs because they didn't choose to leave. They were made to leave, and that seemed different than if they had left on their own. But it's really the same because they broke the habit of us by living away from us. Even if Scout missed me, I don't think that feeling would be strong enough to make him start the journey back to me. He'd have to leave his new life and his new home, and why would he want to do that? No, when something's gone, it's gone, and I think the others are just crazy if they believe anything else.

I did like going out to the woods. I liked how we all stood together and called our dogs' names. I liked that moment when we first arrived, that each evening when we got there we felt hopeful that this might be the evening when the dogs would come back to us. It was like how I used to feel about my father, but it's hard to keep that open. It's like you've got your foot in a door and for a while you can keep the door open, but the door just gets heavier and heavier against your foot and eventually it closes shut on you. There was one day when I couldn't keep my foot in that door any more. There was one day when I no longer believed the dogs would come back and that one last day shut all the other days when I did believe.

I think about Scout in those woods and I'm sure he'd do better than some of those other dogs. He's smart and big and strong, and I've been outside with him a lot. He's good at being outside. He used to chase rabbits and squirrels and get really close to them. I bet it wouldn't take much for him to actually catch them. I'm sure he'd do a lot better than Lily's dog, who lived all the time in that apartment and then had only that small space to go outside at the back of the building. I'm sure Lily's dog wouldn't be able to catch a rabbit. But maybe they share. Maybe Scout would catch a rabbit and share it with the other dogs. I think he is the sort of dog who would do that.

I loved the dog. I'm not afraid to say that. Sometimes it feels as though he is the last thing I will ever love. He waited for me to get home from school. He slept on the end of my bed. I even took beatings for him because I didn't want him to get afraid and be the kind of dog that cringes when someone raises a hand or comes near enough to kick him. I could take a beating for something he'd done and it wouldn't make me afraid the way he would have been if I'd let the beating happen to him. That's why I don't understand why he had to go. All the trouble he got into I blamed on myself. All the trouble I took onto myself, let fall against my own skin. But I suppose it wasn't the trouble, really. It was the fact that I loved Scout that made my stepfather turn against him. The dog had to go because I loved him and my stepfather's hatred of me had to be the strongest thing in the house. His hatred had to be stronger than my love for the dog.

The robbery was never something I wanted to do. It was never something we'd done before. Mostly we went after houses where no one was home, cars that were empty. It was only because Tyler had just bought that gun and wanted to use it. What good was it to have a gun if you couldn't use it to make someone afraid? That's what Tyler thought. That's why he wanted to try a robbery. And because he was older than the rest of us, because he had the car we drove around in, because we were all a little afraid of him—we agreed to what he wanted.

A gas station seemed a good place to rob. You could easily tell when no one was around and there was only ever one person in that booth that you'd have to deal with. You could drive your car right up to the booth so the getting away would be easy. If we had to rob somewhere, it seemed the best sort of place to rob.

Tyler liked that gun a lot. We'd had to go with him in the afternoon that day so he could practise firing it down by the river. We went behind the factory and set up tin cans on the ground for him to shoot at. He wasn't a very good shot, and sometimes he waved the gun around so much, trying to look cool with it, that it went off accidentally. I was nervous of him with that gun, tried to stay well back of him when he was waving it around.

My father used to work in this factory. So did my stepfather. So did Tyler's father, Spencer, and Anson's father and brother. Luke's father worked for the electric company and still has a job, even now.

I can remember coming here in the car with my mother to pick my father up from work; how all the men emptied out of the buildings at the same time; how they walked towards the parking lot with their heads bent down, not speaking. It was like when a wave rides into the shore, how it empties out and then pulls back to fill up again, to reload. Those men were all empty of words and energy and they washed over us and we filled them up again.

When I used to go to the woods with the others and wait for the dogs to come back, it was the same feeling as when we used to wait at the factory for the men to get out of work. Every day it seemed like they wouldn't come back and we waited without speaking, putting all our attention into making the gates open, into seeing the men walk out into the last of the daylight. Maybe this is how dogs feel when they wait for us, that we aren't coming back until we actually appear. Maybe this was how Scout felt, waiting each day for me to come back from school.

Tyler says he can't remember his father at the factory, but Anson waited in a car with his mother, just like I did. We all kept the engines running, I remember the foggy swirls of exhaust breathing out of each car. It's funny to think that Anson and I were here, in this same place, together all that time ago, and now here we are again. It makes me feel good, makes me feel that perhaps everything doesn't just disappear, that some things are circling back, taking the long way, but circling back here towards me.

The river behind the factory is fast and grey. It twists into little knots of water by the banks and sometimes we climb down the muddy slide of grass and push things back into the river that have wedged themselves into the banks. Logs and pieces of picnic tables, planks of wood from bridges and benches, once a wooden crate for oranges.

Tyler threw some tin cans into the river to shoot at, but it was no good. He was a bad shot and the cans bubbled too fast downstream and then were lost forever. Better to set them on the solid ground where he could keep missing them. We would have run out of targets in a minute if we had thrown all the tin cans into the river.

I like to watch the river. When I could relax some about Tyler and the gun, when he was busy reloading or setting the cans back up that he'd somehow managed to hit, I'd walk down to the bank of the river and watch it boil past me. Water has always got something to do. It always seems like it has somewhere important to be going. I wish I could feel like that. I wish I had something to move me the way the river moves what's thrown into it.

My father used to walk me along the river behind the factory when I was small and he still lived with us. He liked how fast the river moved, just like I do, and we would often throw bits of wood into the water and race along the bank, trying to keep up with them as they spun around in the current and tumbled downstream.

"It's never the same water. Think about that," my father said. But I don't know what he meant when he said that. It might not be the same water, but it's the same river. When I throw myself into the water it feels the same as it always did. Every time, it feels exactly the same.

I don't think the other guys think about the river at all. They just use it for swimming and target practice, to throw things in. It does not have its own life.

Tyler was not a good shot and not a good driver. He really shouldn't have been our leader except that he had all the equipment of a leader—he was seventeen, had a weapon and a car. I was just as nervous of his driving as I was when he waved the gun around. He was so excited on the way to the robbery that I thought he'd run off the road, that we'd die before he ever got to stick his gun in someone's face and make them afraid and take their money.

The car that Tyler had to drive was his mother's car and it was full of her stuff—country-music tapes, packages of Kleenex and gum, empty paper coffee cups, hair clips, a tiny pair of running shoes hanging from the rear-view mirror. Tyler was embarrassed about the interior of the car and sometimes he swept all the junk onto the floor in one reckless gesture. But I'd been in the car with him when he was on his way home and I know that he picked the stuff up again and put it back in its proper place before he pulled into his driveway.

The night of the robbery Tyler was so excited that he didn't bother to remove any of his mother's decorations, and as we drove wildly down the highway towards the gas station, I watched the tiny running shoes swing back and forth, fast, from the rear-view mirror. I was sitting in the back of the car and got to feel a little sick from staring so hard at those crazy bobbing shoes.

No one was at the gas pumps and there was just a woman in the booth.

"A woman is good," said Tyler. "A woman will be more afraid than a man."

I didn't think this was necessarily true, but I didn't say anything to Tyler. None of us ever said anything to Tyler. We lurched to a stop by the gas pumps and I got out of the car with the others. I was exhausted from nerves and queasy from watching those little shoes.

The booth was really too small for all of us and we kept knocking things over in there. I had to stop myself from putting the maps back on the rack after we'd spilled it. Anson giggled, but only I heard him. He has a high voice still, like a girl's. It was only when Tyler pulled the gun on the cashier and I looked up to make sure I was out of range of the waving gun that I saw the cashier was Alice.

There are times when life slows down so much that nothing seems to move. It was like that when I watched my father swim away from me on the beach. It's like that when I'm getting hit. The world goes slow and you're stuck in it the way you'd be stuck in mud. This was how it was when I saw Alice and she saw me. In the slow turn of the moment I realized how stupid we were, holding up a gas station; how dangerous Tyler could be; how fucked up things were. I also knew I didn't want Alice to get hurt. I liked her. She had always been kind to me and I didn't want her to get hurt because that asshole, Tyler, couldn't control his enthusiasm for that gun.

I suppose I should have done something. If I'd been a better person, I would have wrestled the gun away from Tyler and made the guys leave. Or I would have argued against robbing anything before we'd even set out that evening. But the truth is that I'm not that good, and when I'm afraid all I do is panic and freeze. Fight or flight, that's how one of my teachers described different animals. A horse is a flight animal because it takes off when it's scared. A wolf will fight. So will a rat. I can't seem to run or fight. I don't know what sort of animal that makes me.

Luckily, someone from outside called the cops and the robbery didn't go any further. There was a mad scramble out of the booth and one awful moment when I had to choose between going with Alice and going with my friends. But I believed Alice when she said they'd be caught. I could see the cops pulling into the gas station and I knew what a bad driver Tyler was and how he'd have no chance in any sort of chase. But more than that, I think I wanted to go with Alice because those evenings we spent out at the edge of the woods calling for the dogs felt more real to me than those nights I broke windows at the factory, or watched the river throw itself down through the middle of this summer. Alice had lost what I'd lost, and that made me trust her in that moment when I had to choose who to follow.

I was glad to be in the cabin again. It was a cool place, all dark and wood-smelling. There were noises around the edges of the walls from small animals trying to get in or out. I felt safe there with Alice, and it was fine really, until that weirdo burst through the door with a speargun.

I can't believe he had a speargun and a hand grenade. Actually, the room with the paintings in it in the farmhouse was full of strange old weapons. I wonder if he had been planning some sort of siege, death stand, barricading himself in and fighting to the last. But he wouldn't really get very far with a rusty speargun and a hand grenade that didn't work. In the room with the paintings there was also a bayonet, a cannonball, and a ball covered with spikes that you whirled around your head.

He was always strange, that Malcolm Dodd. I knew it from the first time I saw him. He had jumpy eyes and a stiff way of moving, like parts of his body could snap off at any moment. He did not seem normal.

Alice was good with the crazy Malcolm. This makes me think she's seen lots of crazy stuff of her own. She talked quietly to him, the way you talk to an animal when it's nervous, and she made him sit down and drink a mug of tea until he calmed down. When she sent me back to the cabin I was glad to go. Those black paintings had freaked me out. They were like windows filled with the darkest, darkest night. It was a darkness that would soak you up.

Alice makes me wash my hands and brush my teeth, and even though I protest, I enjoy the fuss she's making over me. It's been a while since that sort of thing has come my way. My mother would still do that for me, I know she would, but my stepfather doesn't like when she pays more attention to me than she does to him. He's a sensitive man, she said to me once, but I know she means jealous. I don't want my mother to get into trouble, so I tell her not to worry about things that look like they're special efforts just for me. I know that even as I took beatings for Scout, she takes beatings for me.

Alice made me a bed on the floor and I lay there, in the dark, thinking about my friends and wondering what happened to them. Were they caught? Alice said that not much would happen to them if they were, but I'm sure they will be in trouble of some kind. Tyler has that gun, and that's not going to go over well. And what if he was stupid, as usual, and waved it around at the cops and they shot him? For a moment I felt guilty for abandoning them, but then I told myself that I never wanted to rob the gas station in the first place.

And what about me? I'd never been gone overnight before. Would anyone notice? Would my stepfather be angry or glad? Would my mother be worried? I really didn't want to go home to find out. It would be better for my mother if I left. I hoped that Alice would decide to keep me. I decided to be as obliging and helpful as I could so that she'd realize it was a good idea to have me around.

I didn't hear the wolf woman's truck arrive in the morning. I was still asleep, dreaming of Scout. Every night since he left I have dreamed about my dog. Mostly the dreams aren't very exciting, more normal than anything. He's running beside my bike or sleeping on the end of my bed. It doesn't really matter what we're doing because I think the dream is really about the one moment I reach out and touch him and feel that it's all right, he didn't leave, everything is back to how it should be.

So I didn't hear the truck outside the cabin, or if I did, I just stuffed it into the container of my dream. I didn't know anything about the wolf woman being there until Alice was shaking me awake, saying we had to go because someone was trying to shoot the dogs.

That was a strange thing, when she woke me up, because it was like the inside world and the outside world were in the same place. The dogs were in my head and the dogs were in trouble in the real world.

Sometimes now I wonder if I was dreaming Scout, all those nights he wasn't there. Maybe he really did come and visit me while I slept. Animals belong to a different world than we do. Maybe they have the power to appear in places other than where they are. I like to think it was real, all those times I reached out my hand and felt Scout there beside me. I like to think it was real because it's all I have left and it's just too sad to think it might be something out of my head, something I made up.

We got into the wolf woman's truck and drove fast out onto the road. I was still half asleep and couldn't really believe what Alice had told me about the dogs being shot. It all seemed like part of my dream still.

Unlike Tyler, the wolf woman was a good driver. She drove that truck fast, but I never felt worried that we were going to crash. She drove that truck fast and I sat between her and Alice and none of us said a thing.

I don't like the wolf woman. I can't tell Alice this, although I have told her that I don't trust the wolf woman. It's not that she isn't nice. She's nice enough. Maybe she's even too nice. She is always willing to do what Alice wants to do, always agrees with whatever Alice is saying. It's like she's trying too hard. That's what it is. She's trying too hard, and that feels like lying to me.

I don't know what the wolf woman thinks of me. That's the problem with her, you can't tell what she's thinking about anything. She drives the truck with all her attention straight ahead. Even her arms are two straight lines against the steering wheel. Alice, on the other side of me, I can tell is feeling anxious and a little afraid, both for the dogs and of what wolf woman is thinking.

Love is not a good thing, I've decided. It just makes you afraid you'll lose what you love, and then, because your fear makes a space for that to happen, it does. What's the point?

When we get to the fields behind Cooper's farm, to the place we used to wait for the dogs, we get out of the truck. It is a little cold outside, that thin sort of cold of early morning. Steam rises from the hood of the truck. The grass is slippery with dew when I step out onto it.

I think we all see the hunters at the same time. They come out of the woods, in the very spot where we were always hoping the dogs would emerge from. The first few men are wearing orange vests and carrying guns. They don't speak to each other or to us. I recognize Anson's father and the other men look familiar too. I think they are all men who used to work with my father at the factory.

One of the men has something draped around his neck. Another man carries something in his arms. When he gets closer I can see that it's a dog. A dead dog. My dog.

Scout never liked to be carried, that's what I think first. He was too big for that, felt himself too big for that, and always struggled if you tried to pick him up.

"There's my dog," I say to Alice. "There's Scout."

His fur is smeared over with blood. His head is twisted sideways and hangs over the arm of the hunter.

I rush at the man carrying Scout. "That's my dog," I yell, and I reach up to pull Scout from his arms. Scout's fur is cool, as cool as the morning. He has become the morning by dying in it.

The hunter pushes my hands away. "I'm sorry," he says. "We need to keep the dogs for evidence." He stopped walking when I rushed up to him, but he starts again now.

"Evidence for what?" I say, but then I see what the last man in the group, Tyler's father, has in his arms. Lily. She is stuck all over with mud and leaves and yet she still has that sweater buttoned up to her neck.

They've shot her in the head. They thought Lily was a dog and they've shot her in the head. I'm sorry I ever teased her. I'm sorry I thought she was stupid. Lily was braver than all of us. She became a dog and they shot her in the head.

When the hunters have passed through the field, on their way to the farmhouse, we get back into the truck and we just sit there without driving off. Wolf woman puts her head against the steering wheel. They shot her dog too. He was the dog draped around the shoulders of the first hunter. Wolf woman's dog was huge. His wolf head was as wide across as a basketball.

I feel ashamed, but I can't help myself. I wrap my head in my arms and I start to cry, harder than I've ever cried before. I feel like I'm dying. Alice rubs my back gently, the way my mother used to when I was small and I'd thrown up. Alice rubs my back, and I'm too tired and sad to think about minding.

On the drive back to the cabin no one speaks. It's just like on the drive to the woods, only much worse because now we know what happened to the dogs. On the drive to the woods all things were still open. Now everything has closed down.

I feel bad for crying when neither Alice or wolf woman has cried, so I don't look at them as we drive back. I watch the hood of the truck and the road that reels out in front of it. When we get back, wolf woman drives up to the cabin but doesn't shut the engine off.

"I have to go tomorrow," she says.

"Go?" says Alice.

"Back to work. Everything I needed to do here at the university I've done."

"But you'll be back."

"No," says wolf woman. "I won't."

I hate her for having this conversation while I'm trapped between her and Alice, and I know she's doing it on purpose. She wants me here because it will prevent Alice from making a scene. Alice wouldn't want to make a scene in front of me. And it's working. All poor Alice can do is to repeat everything wolf woman says in a kind of dumb, flat way.

"You told me this," she says, and her voice is shaking a bit now. "Did you? When?"

Wolf woman doesn't say anything. The truck engine thumps and rattles. Alice opens the passenger door.

"Come on," she says to me. "You'll be back and we'll talk, right?" she says to wolf woman.

"Okay," says wolf woman, but I know she's lying. I think Alice knows it too. She pulls on my arm and I slide along the seat and drop down to the ground beside her. The truck is in reverse even before Alice has slammed the door shut.

Everything is lost. I feel it in that moment. And the terrible thing is that the space something takes up when it's around is still there when it's gone, only now it's filled with nothing. It's filled with missing.

"Come on," I say to Alice, because she's just standing there, watching the truck reverse down the driveway.

And then there's Malcolm, running towards us. He must have heard the truck drive up, or been watching for it. He's wearing the same clothes as yesterday.

"Sorry," he says, when he's close to us. "I'm sorry about last night."

And suddenly I hate him too. His dog wasn't one of the ones the hunters shot. He didn't lose anything.

"They killed my dog," I say to him. "They killed Lily." And then I can't stop saying it. "They killed my dog. They killed Lily." And I must be yelling because Malcolm looks scared and stops coming towards us, and Alice puts her hand on my shoulder and tells me to quiet down.

"I'm not yelling," I say.

"You are," she says.

Malcolm trots back to his house and I let Alice lead me to the cabin. The morning has come undone, that's how it feels. The morning has come undone and all the worst things, the things there are to be afraid of, have spilled out into this day.

Now we sit here at this table in the cabin. Alice is trying not to cry, but it's not working very well. There's nothing I can think of to say to her because I hate everything at this moment and I'm afraid, if I have to say things I don't feel, that I will start to hate her as well.

The cabin roof creaks and I realize that the morning sun must be drying out the shingles and those creaks are the sound of the flaps of wood shrinking in the heat.

"We'll have to do something about you," says Alice, but she says it so flatly that she might as well be talking about some chore she doesn't want to be doing.

"What?" I say, and I feel angry with her too. It has happened. I hate them all.

Alice looks at me. "I don't know," she says, and she gets up from the table and goes over to the bed. She lies down, turning on her side away from me, and I can see the rhythmic shaking of her shoulders and know that she's crying, and it's like her crying is an engine that's driving her whole body forward.

The sun angles through the window behind me and makes long spears of light on the surface of the table. I don't belong here. I don't know these people. The thing between us has gone. Murdered. Lily is dead. Scout is dead.

I get up from the table quietly and walk across the floor of the cabin without Alice noticing. The door creaks a little, but I get through undetected. Outside, the sun touches the side of my face as I step off the porch and I feel a little better, more certain about what I am doing.

There is no point wanting something different, or remembering how things used to be. If you have hope, it is only hunted down and brought back with blood, thick as jam, coating its lovely fur.

There is nothing to believe in.

I will go home, and take my punishment like a man.

lily

First I call, and then I stop. First I run, and then I walk.

The trees are like dark spears of flame, each one licked about with red and orange. Am I going out of the fire, or into it? This is what I can never remember. Who am I there to save?

Dog.

I wish I had *before* back. When I try to think about it, it's like pulling at a dream. There are no details, but I can feel that it happened. I am tugging and tugging at my mind and nothing tugs back.

Now there's just walking and the light running out in front of me and the prickle bushes sticking my arms and face.

But *before* doesn't want me back, maybe that's the problem. Maybe it's like Dog and ran off and doesn't want to be caught. Maybe it ran into these woods, back and back, and even though I'm coming back into this house, I won't be able to find the baby.

Dog. It's not the baby, it's Dog.

Everyone will be worried, and no one will care. Lily isn't gone. Lily isn't there.

If I look up, I see a net of heaven, and if I look down, I see a net of earth. Cords of green and brown above me and below.

The light comes down like smoke and I trip over the cords on the ground as I hurry. I am in a hurry. It doesn't smell like fire, that is what I must remember. If it doesn't smell like fire, it isn't. The fire was hot and sharp where it raced across my skin. I could see it coming at me in a line of smoky orange.

This was before Dog. Dog was to make me feel better after the fire and the hospital. Dog lay on the end of my bed and we were happy. Once I woke in the night and saw my mother putting things from my room into a big green bag.

"What are you doing?" I said.

"You won't need these any more," she said, so quietly that Dog didn't even wake up.

She was putting books into that big green bag. My mother was putting in all my books that had words inside them.

I am tugging and tugging at my mind and nothing tugs back.

I don't know how long I've been gone now. I keep listening to my breathing or my feet scuffing along the ground, and I forget to call her name.

Dog. Dog.

My breathing sounds wet and wheezy, dry and breezy. It comes in the space between the shuffle of my feet. It is like music, and then I walk into something spiky and the music all deflates out of me.

I must have gone for miles now, but everything in the middle looks the same as on the edge. I touch the dark bodies of the trees as I pass them and their skin is warm from the day. I stop and listen for their breathing, to see if it sounds like mine, but theirs is high up and rustly, doesn't make a sound all the time like mine does.

What if Dog went out the other side of this wood? What if the other side is like the first side, one great big field, and when I get there I won't know how to get home because it won't be in the same place as the first field, even though it might look the same?

Where am I?

If I look at my shoes, I don't feel so afraid. And if I look at my shoes, I don't trip over the net spread across the earth. But it's not so good now. I wish I hadn't come. I'm hungry and I don't like being spiked by all the spiky things and I can't see a way out. *Look at your shoes. Look only at your shoes.*

The worst thing about thinking about when it used to be different is knowing that what used to be different was me.

The baby grew up. His name is Michael and he doesn't live with us any more. Sometimes when he comes to visit he seems so big and like a man that I don't see how he can believe that I carried him out of that fire. He looks at me as if he can't believe it, and then I have to tell him, tell all of them.

"I carried you out," I say. "I carried you out of that fire. You would have died without me."

"Shush, Lily," they all say. Shush, shush.

Shush, Lily.

I sit down with my back up against the warm skin of a tree. I sit down and hold my knees, which feels a little better, and cry, which feels a lot worse.

Shush, Lily.

The sound in the forest is the sound of me. The light comes down like smoke and the trees are straight with waiting and the sound that fills us all up is me.

* * *

There's a pushing at my head and something wet against my ear and the smell all around me like dirt and food that's gone bad. I open my eyes and the dogs are there. They circle around me and the tree. When I put out my hands I feel their dusty fur and they lean into me when I touch them. They lean into me so that I will touch them.

Dog is there, with the same eyes that I remember and a kind of smiling look that happens when she opens her mouth.

"Dog," I say, and she comes right up to me and pushes her face into mine and licks me on the nose.

There are a lot of them. They go around me and the tree and then they go out from there, into the trees, past where I can see clearly. They go around and around, and when I stand up they push against each other and against me and we move like that, like the circle that pulses out when you drop a stone into the water.

I am very glad to see them and I tell them that. "I thought I'd never find you," I say. "I thought you'd gone out the other side and I was lost and alone in here."

The dogs take me with them. They know where they're going and I follow them. Some of them still wear collars around their necks, and if I stumble on the ground, I can reach out and hold onto one of the collars.

There's a grey dog and a wolf dog and an orange dog with crazy, fluffy hair. I can't remember their names, but they don't need their names here. I can't make them do anything here using their names. Even Dog, who knows me, doesn't need to be mine like she had to be when she lived in the apartment and slept on the end of my bed. She is not mine here. I am hers.

Lily is a dog. Lily is a dog. Lily is a dog.

*   *   *

They live far into the forest. I think it must be all the way into the middle. They live in a big hole they've made under two fallen logs. They've dug down so that the logs make a kind of roof and it's cosy in there with all the dogs smashed up against me like pillows of fur. They let me sleep in the middle of them because I am the new dog, and because I don't have any fur and at night it gets cold and I need to cuddle up to them. They let me cuddle up to them, even the dogs who don't know me. They are kind.

I sleep with them and I am not afraid. The dogs are warm and they make little groans when they sleep and the breath runs out of them and sometimes they kick out their legs, but if I put a hand on their heads, they stop. The dogs make a knot around me and it feels good to be tied up with them so snug.

I cannot eat what they eat because it is bloody and still stuck with fur. It used to be a rabbit or a squirrel. They rip it to pieces and sometimes Dog or the big wolf brings me a bit and drops it on the ground by my feet. Then it is bloody and stuck with fur and covered in dirt. I am too hungry but I can't eat. My stomach whistles with hunger. My tongue glues itself to the top of my mouth.

There is a pond in the forest, not far from where the dogs sleep under the logs, and they took me there to drink. I got down on my hands and knees at the edge and I drank with my mouth in the water, like they do, and it was a good way to drink. I could drink and wash my face at the same time.

I wish I knew how to make a fire because I think that cooking the meat the dogs brought home would help me. I used to know how to make a fire. I made a fire and it burned the house down and I ran out with the baby and I wore a cape of lickety flame. It's a good thing, then, I don't have matches. I would burn the forest down and have to carry the dogs out, and I think they're a lot heavier than the baby was. But what I sometimes do is make a pretend fire with sticks, while the dogs are out hunting. I make it just in front of the sleeping place so we could lie in bed and watch the pretty flames. I pile the sticks together. I stamp them out.

Sometimes there is a hungry time for the dogs, when they don't bring rabbits or squirrels back for many nights. When this happens they go out of the woods for a longer time, and when they come back they bring something much bigger than a rabbit or squirrel and they eat until their bellies are bursting, and then they sleep for a long time. The big pieces of meat have curls of hair still attached to them. I think the big pieces of meat used to be sheep.

I think sometimes that I should make the dogs come home with me, but I don't know how to get there, and I don't think they do either, and so, even though I think this, I never do anything about it. My parents seem very far away now. So does the bus I used to ride out to the woods, and all those people I used to wait with at the edge of the trees. I remember their voices calling out the names of their dogs, how their voices sounded like the church bells across the street from my apartment—all different notes playing at the same time. That's what I remember, their voices, and how they walked up and down in a line like soldiers or people in the supermarket. They might be the ones who know where I've gone. They would be the only ones who know where I've gone.

I didn't think I'd ever live in the woods, that I'd ever be one dog in a pack of dogs, but I like it. I'm happy with the dogs and they seem happy with me. I don't talk as much with them. It's easy to figure out what they mean without using words. They don't speak with words anyway, so it seems silly to do that now. My voice can do other things than words. It can make the noises the dogs make, little whines and yelps and groans. These are good noises. They say as much as any word can say.

At night sometimes the moon is bright like a headlight. It shines a tunnel of white through the forest and it makes me feel like jumping up from the bed of dogs and following it into the trees. I think the light has come to lead me home and once I scrambled up to follow it, but one of the dogs growled at me and I knew I wasn't allowed to leave the nest. The dogs have rules for me. Some of these are the same rules I used to have for Dog. No getting up if no one else is getting up. No going anywhere on your own. Sometimes it seems the dogs are more strict with me than I ever was with Dog. Sometimes I'm not sure they like me, but then one of them will nudge me with his head and I'll scratch behind his ears and he'll make the noise that says he's happy with what I'm doing. It's best when I don't think too much about anything else. It's best when I'm just glad to be a dog and to do what the rest of the dogs are doing.

Fur and claws. Ears and paws. Teeth and jaws. Fur and claws. Ears and paws. Teeth and jaws.

When the dogs sleep they roll into a ball and press that ball against me. I have to be careful about how I fall asleep because once the dogs are all squished around me I won't be able to move, even if I want to. In the beginning I curled up in a ball like the other dogs, but now I take up as much room as I can at first, even sticking my arms out at my sides, because I know that dogs make the room shrink in the night, all fastened around me as they like to be. I am like one of those long doughnuts I used to like to eat, and the dogs are like those round doughnuts, and that's how we sleep.

Sometimes, after the dogs have eaten, they like to play. They will chase each other through the woods, or fight over a stick. Once they played tug-of-war with a squirrel tail. If we're down by the pond and the dogs get hot from playing, they will throw themselves into the water, flop down in it, and rise covered in a green veil of scum. The orange fluffy dog looks like a small dog when he gets wet. His nice curls flatten and he looks all slick and skinny. He is one of the fastest runners and he catches a lot of squirrels.

I like when the dogs are playing in the pond. The water is all greeny and the light coming through the trees shows the bugs and weeds on the surface, shows a sort of dust above the surface. There are turtles on the logs that cross the pond. Once there were six turtles on one log. I count them up and I tell the dogs how many, even though the dogs don't care. They are not much interested in turtles. They are not much interested in the snakey-snakes either. Or the frogs. I have been practising making a noise like a frog, and I am getting quite good at it. The other night I did it for a long time in the nest, until one of the dogs growled at me to be quiet. But I was so good at the frog noise that other frogs had started to answer me back. I wonder what I was saying to them.

The wolf dog is the leader of the dogs. He is big and scary-looking and he is mostly kind, except when he isn't. He isn't if another dog, or me, tries to eat before he does. He isn't if another dog, or me, wants to play with him when he is rest-ing. Then he growls and snaps and you have to lie down in front of him to show him that you're afraid. Sometimes I am not even pretending when I lie down on the ground and turn my head away from him. I am afraid.

The wolf dog has a favourite dog that he has married. It looks a lot like him, but it is smaller and its head is not as wide. They go everywhere together and sleep touching each other. No other dog can come up to the wolf dog's favourite dog without him growling them away. I think it is very hard to be the wolf dog because he has to take care of so much. It is worse than being a parent because there are so many dogs. Sixteen. There are sixteen dogs. I counted them the first night we were all lying together in the nest.

There is no way I could ever be the leader of the dogs. I am not smart enough. And in that other world people are always thinking themselves the leaders of the dogs, but I'm not sure they are really smart enough either. Maybe it's because there are so many machines in that world and dogs don't know how to work machines. But I bet they could learn if they had lessons. They are quick learners.

How long have I been here? I can't remember what it was like before I came here. This world is not like that other world. I know many new things.

I know that a dog can catch a mouse. I have seen the greeny light of the pond shine through the trees like a lantern. I have watched an owl turn his head all the way around to look at me. I have seen how darkness turns to milk and that milky light becomes the new day. I have seen snakey-snakes tied together in a knot in the sun. I know what the bones of a rabbit look like, and the bones of a groundhog, and the bones of a squirrel. I have seen turtles arranged like buttons on a log. I have seen the moon and the stars and a night when there was nothing caught in the net of heaven.

I know the difference between the growl of hunger and the growl of anger. I know that a rabbit screams as it dies. A leaf makes a soft scuff when it falls to the ground. I have heard all the noise of night and all the noise of day. They do not hold the same noises. I know the noise of the splash a turtle makes in a pond when it slides off a log. I have heard six turtles slide off that log, one after the other. I have heard the owl ask, "Who cooks for you?" and the frog reply, "Enid. Enid." I have heard the wind at play and the wind at war. I listen to the soft talking of rain on the logs over my head, and my own slow heart beating down.

I have smelt the breath of dogs, their wet and muddy fur—fur dusty with dried pond slime, fur sticky with blood. I know the smell of the earth after rain and the smell of dawn. I have smelt my body become as fragrant as the bodies of the dogs. I know that fear smells like old blood and the tin sky that happens before a storm. I know the difference between living and dead flesh. I have smelt the world green again.

I have tasted the water where the frogs live. I have tasted the plants that grow around the den and most of them are too bitter to keep in my mouth. I have drunk the sweet falling rain and tasted the dew. Once I ate the plump purple wriggle of a worm.

I have touched the fur and faces and bones of the animals I live beside. I know the earth with the heat still in it and the earth grown cold without the day, the slippery skin of logs when they're wet. I have put my hand in the light on the earth that is made by the moon, and touched my own body and felt it new again.

There is a silence that opens and opens out from me, that separates me from everything that came before, and sometimes I can forget that when I snuggle against the warm bellies of the dogs, touch their watery noses and the secret place between their shoulders that makes them rub their heads against me.

I don't know what wakes me. A sound. I lie there, with the dogs curled close around me. It is almost the night still, almost the day, that dirty time between, when darkness starts to drain away.

I am not the only one awake. Dog has stirred beside me, opens her eyes. We look at each other and she stiffens her ears up on her head to listen better. There's the sound again. Now I know what it is. Something I haven't heard for a long time now. A man's voice.

Then all the dogs are awake, awake and bristling with anger. No, I try to say to them. People are good. But I seem to have lost my words. I open my mouth to speak and I make the sound of the frog. *Enid. Enid.*

It happens so quickly. The men come through the trees. They are coloured like the leaves and carrying guns. They wear boots and some of them have hats on. The dogs start to growl and they back up against the fallen logs. They do not want the men to come near the nest. The men stop. I think they have understood, and then they raise the guns to their shoulders and the noise is the most terrible noise I've ever heard, terrible and close. They shoot wolf dog and he squirms on the ground, yelping like a puppy. They shoot him again and he is quiet. Dog, who is right next to me and has put her body in front of mine, has been shot through the ear. There's blood trickling down her lovely black fur into her eye.

I wave my hands. I open my rusty voice, and I make, finally, a human word.

"Hello," I say.

spencer

We met up at Cooper's farm on Friday night. The idea was to sleep there so we could make an early start the next morning, without having to wait for guys who were late or didn't show. Now, of course, that doesn't seem to have been the best idea.

No, I wouldn't say I was hungover on Saturday morning, but there had been a lot of drinking on Friday night. Mostly beer. Some of the guys were doing shots of bourbon, but I stuck mostly to beer. I went to bed drunk, but I go to bed drunk most nights now. I'm used to drinking beer, if you know what I mean. It sounds a stupid thing to say, but I'm good at it. I know when to stop so that I won't get sick. I know how I'll feel after any given number of beers. How many? Probably a dozen. That's what I came with and I always finish what I start. It's not unusual, that's what I'm trying to say. I was not more drunk than usual, and I didn't have a hangover the next morning—well, nothing I'd recognize as a hangover. I'm always a little slow in the morning until after I've had my coffee.

The whole thing was Tommy Cooper's idea. The dogs had been killing his sheep and he had petitioned the city council, and since they were slow to act and hadn't decided what to do, he wanted to address the problem himself. Those are his words—*address the problem*—you can quote me on that. Yes, *address the problem* meant shoot the dogs. He called up half a dozen of us who played cards with him on occasion and he asked us if we'd help him out. Hunting season is still a few weeks away, but I was eager for it, and when Tommy called, I didn't hesitate. Hunting season is the only thing I've been looking forward to all year. Since I've been laid off from the factory the days stretch endlessly ahead of me, and I have no real sense of what to do with them.

In the end there were six of us who went into the woods after the dogs. Stan couldn't make it. His wife was having another baby. They already have four children. He sounded pissed off when he called me, like he'd rather be going hunting with us than having to take his wife to the hospital. I know how it is. Family stuff is so depressing. The police arrested my son, Tyler, on Friday night. I was late getting to Tommy Cooper's because I had to go and pick him up from the police station. He'd tried to rob a gas station. Attempted robbery, and a weapons charge because he had got himself a gun. Now I'm going to have to hire a lawyer to keep him out of jail. He's got a court date, and they won't be lenient. The robbery charge probably wouldn't have stuck because it's his first offence, but they'll come down hard about the gun. The stupid little shit. As if I don't have enough to worry about.

Angry? No, I don't think I was particularly angry. I mean, no more than usual. I was angry at Tyler, but I also didn't want to deal with him, so I let my wife take care of it. I went to the police station and brought him home and after that he was her problem.

My life is just crap, that's all. I certainly wasn't angry at the dogs, if that's what you mean. Tommy Cooper was angry at the dogs. He'd seen them corner a sheep and tear the flesh from it while it was still alive and bawling. They will do that, wild dogs. They don't kill cleanly like a wolf. Wolves will go for the jugular and the animal will die fast, but wild dogs just attack in a kind of frenzy, and they don't concern themselves with the killing of the animal. They are intent on getting the meat. It is horrible to watch something under your care die so painfully. This is what Tommy Cooper had seen happen to his sheep. This is why he hated the dogs and wanted them dead. He was angry at the city council too, for being so slow to act. It's not as though there haven't been other complaints about the dogs. Other farms have had their livestock raided. The dogs have been seen out by the dump, spreading garbage through the fields and across the dump road. And there was that woman who was attacked by them out there. I remember seeing the pictures in the paper. Tommy planned to shoot the dogs and lay their bodies on the steps of city hall. He thought that would show the council they couldn't ignore the problem.

Did I think that was a good idea? No, not really. I could see the need to do something about the dogs, but it seemed a bit dramatic to lay their corpses on the steps of city hall. I mean, the problem would have already been addressed when that happened. What was the point in making a point after the situation had already been taken care of? But then, they weren't my sheep. I hadn't watched them being ripped apart. I hadn't heard them scream. I suppose Tommy Cooper was so angry that his anger went past the dogs. Killing them wasn't enough to satisfy the way he felt. He needed to be angry with more than just the dogs.

If I had to do it over, of course, I wouldn't have gone at all. But there are so many things I wouldn't have done at all in my life. So, you see, maybe I'm not capable any more of making a good decision. I've often thought that, and especially these days. Was it a good idea to marry someone because she was pretty and because she wanted to escape her parents and I felt sorry for her and wanted to help? Was it a good idea to have had a family when my position at the factory was always, at best, unstable? I mean, I wasn't really good at any one thing and they bounced me from department to department. I always knew it was just a matter of time before I was let go completely. They only kept me there for that long because of my father.

It's funny, but I always wanted to work in that factory. I know it's not very ambitious or anything, to have wanted that since I was a child, but I did. My father worked there. This was back in the days when the factory was doing well, back when the men worked with their hands rather than with machines. It would have been quieter in those days. I often thought of that, how in my father's time you would have been able to hear the making of the furniture, that the tables would have been planed by hand, the table legs turned by hand. No one I worked with knew how to do this sort of work any more. Even cars now are operated by computers, and to be fixed they have to be hooked up to other computers. Mechanics are now "diagnosticians," that's the word they use. But in my father's time they knew how to make things by hand. They knew what hands were for.

I would sometimes go to the factory with my father when I was a boy. I would climb the hills of sawdust out by the lumberyard and pick up the little bits of wood that nobody needed any more. I would hammer these bits of wood together and make boats to float down the river behind the factory. Often I had hammered too many pieces of wood together and the boat I made rolled upside down and dropped to the bottom of the river. But once in a while one of these boats would wobble through the current and make it all the way downstream to the train bridge.

I liked the smell of the sawdust and the smell of the cut wood. I liked how all the men knew my father by name, that they called out to him as we walked past them. I liked how every man in that building, and there were probably two hundred men in that building, knew me by name as well. This meant that my father talked about me when he was at work, that he was proud of me.

My father told a lot of stories about the factory, but there's one story I particularly remember. In the early days the only heating in the building was from the forge that was part of the factory workings. The building was drafty because it was right on the river, and in the winters it was as freezing cold inside as outside. The men would warm their tools in the fire of the forge on those winter mornings, to keep their hands from stiffening up with cold. They heated their tools and then they worked with them, and the heat from the steel kept their hands warm.

No, I don't suppose any of this has much to do with what happened on Saturday morning.

We got up before dawn. Tommy's wife made us coffee and eggs. No one talked much at breakfast. The downstairs, where we'd slept on the floor, still smelled of beer. It was stronger even than the smell of coffee, and I ate quickly because I just wanted to be away from the farmhouse and outside where I could breathe fresh air.

We had all been hunting together before, and we'd often been into those woods behind Cooper's farm after deer. We cleaned the guns and loaded them and set off across the fields. There was still not much talking. I never like to talk when I'm hunting anyway. It disturbs my concentration. I like to notice the world around me, feel the weather on my skin, watch the ground for signs of deer. I don't want to be operating from inside my head, where words are. I want to be operating from my body. My body in the body of the world.

I don't remember the order in which we crossed the field, or the order in which we entered the woods. Once we were in the woods we fanned out between the trees, but remained in visual contact with one another. Our plan was to be in the woods early enough in the morning to surprise the dogs while they were still in their den.

I remember how good the woods smelled, starting to absorb the first bit of heat from the sun, how that released the smells of the trees and the leaves and the rich scent of the earth itself. It's always a surprise to encounter something and have it be better than you remembered, like you've had to remember it as less than it was in order to be able to live with the lack of it. I had forgotten how much I loved to be in the woods, how good it made me feel to step quietly out into the morning.

What was my life that I could forget the one thing that made me feel good? It was doing crosswords and drinking beer in the evenings on my own or with some of the other guys from the factory who'd been laid off with me. Maybe this was a waste of time, but I did like the crosswords. I liked finding the right word for a space and then using that word as a hook to hang other words on. But that was all I liked. Since I've been out of work I've had to cook the food and wash the clothes, be there when the kids come home from school, because my wife is working overtime to try to keep us afloat. It pisses me off to have her out there earning our living and then coming home and giving me shit because the house isn't tidy enough for her liking. I know she is doing her best, but I was never meant to be a house-wife. When we married we agreed that she would be the one to stay home with the kids. I'm not a new sort of man. I don't get satisfaction from ironing or putting groceries away. I liked my family a lot better when I could leave them behind in the morning and return to them again at night.

I never really got on with Tyler. He was a whiny baby, and when he could walk he was always getting in my way. Underfoot, just like a cat. I swear I even stepped on him a couple of times by accident. It's a terrible thing to say, but I don't think I've ever liked him. He's always either whining or bragging, and I can't stand either of those things in a per-son. I mostly try to stay out of his way because I just end up angry at him and I hate how that feels. I get along much better with my daughter.

Back to the story? Isn't this part of the story?

Okay.

We walked for a while through those woods. We found

some dog scat and saw all the small bones in it and knew they must be living on a diet of rodents and squirrels. No wonder they wanted to go after Tommy's sheep. They were probably starving to death. I didn't say this out loud though, as Tommy was with us and eager to get even for his murdered sheep. But I had nothing against the dogs, really I didn't. They were just trying to survive. I didn't begrudge them their survival. I wasn't keen to kill them, but I was keen to hunt them. Sometimes you forget one thing in the shadow of the other. You forget that hunting is about killing. So I tried to remember that as we stepped quickly and quietly through those woods. I tried to remember that this would be the last morning those dogs would be alive, and I tried to notice everything on their behalf. I tried to be—what's the word?—I tried to be reverent about knowing this was the last morning they would spend on this earth. That's what a good hunter does. He has respect for what he kills. He even feels sad that he has to kill it. But the killing of the dogs was set in place by the act of hunting. I enjoyed the hunting too much to give it up.

When I walked through the woods I thought about the dogs in their den, curled around the last little scrap of the night. I thought of how those dogs used to belong to people, used to sleep on the ends of beds, or on soft rugs on the floor. They used to eat out of bowls that said "Dog" on the side. What would kill the dogs in that life would be accidental, or the slow running down of their bodies. They didn't need to be wary of danger in that old life, and yet, were they? Were their wild instincts in place then? Is that why they could turn so quickly? Were they never who they appeared to be?

I don't know what any of the other men were thinking. As I said, we didn't talk on our walk through the woods. Perhaps they were thinking similar things to what I was thinking. We have had, after all, similar lives. We were a pack, just like the dogs, bound together by circumstance and need and habit. We were perhaps thinking and feeling many of the same things, and yet, I bet when you talk to each of them, they'll have completely different stories from each other and from me. That's the trouble with words. They sometimes set you out on a course you never intended. It is very easy to choose the wrong word.

There are words in my life that I wish I'd never said. I wish I'd never told my wife that I loved her, because then I had to line up all my actions with those words. I had to always act like that was true. And those three words, *I love you*, should never be used if you don't mean them. My lying has meant I will never get to use them on anyone else. I went against my own truth, my own heart, and there is really no coming back from that.

No, I'm not lying about anything that happened on that Saturday morning. What would be the point? The other people there will tell other stories, but they will all agree on one point—I was the one who shot that girl. I can't back away from that. And I don't want to. My life has collapsed, but maybe it needed to collapse. Of course, I wish it hadn't happened this way, but I can see now that it would have happened some other way. There was nothing holding me together. I could only come apart.

We came on the dogs almost by accident. They had left a loose trail of scat and prints, but we had expected them to be farther into the centre of the woods. They had made their den under fallen logs in a clearing not far from the pond we sometimes come across in hunting season. The pond where the deer sometimes come down and drink. I remember us all getting to the clearing at roughly the same time. I know I was the one who came out of the trees and was directly facing the den. I think Tommy was on one side of me. I can't remember who was on the other side of me.

There were more dogs than I'd thought. They woke up as soon as we approached the clearing, growling and standing their ground before us. They far outnumbered us, and even though we had the guns, there was a moment when I was afraid of the dogs.

There was a huge dog that challenged us, didn't act afraid at all. It looked exactly like a wolf. Tommy shot it first. It is always a good idea to take the leader out. This works in any situation. It screws up the group if they lose their leader right away. The big wolf dog was shot first, and then a skinny one that looked to be part collie. Someone tried to kill a black dog, but only shot it through the ear. I had my gun raised, but I hadn't shot anything yet. A few of the dogs had run off into the woods at the first sound of the guns. The other guys fired after them and I heard yelping, so I assume some of them were hit.

The dogs had unwound themselves from sleep. They had stood up and taken a stand at the rear of the den, growling and trying to stare us down. But there was something else in the den. It wasn't a dog. I think I knew that from the beginning. But it was wild. I knew that too. It struggled to get upright. It was waving and moaning and starting to come towards me. Then it made a screeching sound and I shot it.

When it was dead I knew it was human because as it fell its limbs flung out at its sides and I could see that they were arms. I could see that the tangle of fur was really hair. When the body lay still on the ground, bleeding onto it, I could see the human legs and back. I could see the little knots of spine at the neck and the unclenched hands.

"Fuck," said Tommy. "That's a girl."

We carried a couple of the dead dogs out for evidence, to prove our reason for being in the woods that morning. We took the dogs that were the most impressive—the wolf dog and a fierce-looking pit bull. We left the other dead dogs in their den. We left them where they fell, sprawled out on the dirt as though they were sleeping.

I carried the dead girl out of the woods myself. She was still warm, and not that heavy. She lay in the sling of my arms all floppy and relaxed, like a sleeping child that is lifted from the back seat of a car and carried up to bed. She was dirty and smelled bad, earthy, like something that had been buried and then dug up.

I had shot her in the head and I tried not to look at the crushed cheekbone or the ear that flapped against the side of her skull, or the eye socket that was compressed back into her brain. The other side of her face was really quite pretty. She had a nice mouth and a nice high forehead. She wore a grubby sweater and blue jeans, and nothing on her feet. They swung slowly back and forth as I walked, those naked, dirty feet. I tried not to look at them, or at her face, as I carried her through the woods and then across the fields towards Cooper's farm.

It was strange, carrying her body. I was holding her so close to me that she could have been my child, or my girl-friend. She could have been someone I loved.

At first I thought the dogs had somehow caught her, that she was their prey and they were going to kill and eat her. But her clothes were too dirty for this. She had been living with the dogs. And when I saw her in the den she had been waking up with the dogs, in the midst of the dogs, as one of the dogs.

Later I found out that she was retarded. Well, not retarded, but she had brain damage from some childhood accident. Then I think that maybe that's why the dogs took her in, because they knew she was weak and needed protection.

But at the time I knew nothing about her. I thought she was a normal person and I wondered why the dogs had decided to let her join them and why she had decided to stay with them. The dogs were so defensive with us, and I know they have attacked before. What was in the girl that was special? For that's how I thought of it, that she must have had something in her that set her apart from the rest of us. And what was in her that would make her choose the dogs over human company?

I thought about all this later, after I'd carried the body of the girl out of the woods and across the fields to Cooper's farm.

When we came across the field the sun was farther up into the sky. My feet slid on the dew covering the grass and I could see the shimmer over the field where the cool of the early morning was rising to meet the heat of the day. Near the edge of the field there was a pickup truck and two women and a boy standing beside it. As we went past the boy rushed at Sam, who was carrying the dead pit bull, and tried to pull the dog from his arms. He said it was his dog, and I believed him, he was that upset, but there was nothing we could do, not now, and so we moved past the women and the boy without speaking to them. I had forgotten that the dogs in the woods had once belonged to people. No, I hadn't forgotten that. What I had forgotten was that there were people who had once belonged to those dogs.

There was a slight breeze coming across the field as we walked towards the farm. I remember this because I remember that the hair of the dead girl lifted a little with each movement of air. She went before me into the morning, that was what I thought, that she was dead but she still experienced the changes of the day. She was still *there*.

I haven't been able to sleep since I shot that girl. I lie awake in the dark, afraid that if I do fall asleep, I will wake up and it will be that morning again. I will have to get up and go into the woods after the dogs. I will have to kill that girl all over again.

My wife says I'm too restless and she can't get enough sleep with my tossing and turning, so I've moved to the living-room couch. I lie awake there, watching the street-lights outside the window, how each light softens out into darkness. How each light is its own planet.

I know I should feel sad, but I don't feel anything. Some nights I can't believe it has happened, that I could do such a thing, and some nights it seems I couldn't escape from it. Both things seem true.

I have never been wild. I never wanted to be, and yet my life has grown wild around me. I suppose there might always have to be that balance, and if wildness is not happening within you, then it's happening outside of you. Is it always to be feared as I fear it? Is the only choice either to be the wild thing or to shoot at the wild thing? I think so. There is no living safely with wildness. If you let a wild thing into your house, it tears everything to pieces.

Why did I shoot? That's the real question, isn't it? That's what everyone wants to know.

This is what I tell myself is true: I shot out of panic because I was afraid of the dogs and I was afraid of the creature moving towards me. I shot because the others had started shooting. I shot because I was carrying the gun and it was loaded and it was what I was there for.

But the thing I know to be true is also there, curled up with these excuses, and I can't run from it. It rises, snarling and defiant, staring me down.

I shot the girl, not because I thought she was a dog, but because I knew she was a woman.

malcolm

It was the fault of the painting. Before that everything was under control. Well, perhaps it wasn't really under control, but it was familiar enough to feel under control. There was a pattern to my days that felt comfortable. But the painting undid all of that.

I had spent years not painting. Not doing something takes up as much time as doing it, more perhaps because your failure to act takes up a lot of space in your thoughts. It takes up all your thoughts, really. Years of not painting drove me crazy. How would I ever know how good I could have been? Perhaps all my best painting would have happened in those years of not painting. What if not painting had destroyed my gift forever? On and on it went like this, day after day, night after night. I walked from room to room, trying to drive these thoughts out of my head, and all that happened was that I tired myself out with the pacing, and the loneliness whistled around me, and I ended up sprawled on the couch, drinking again. I'd wake up in the morning feeling groggy and sorry for myself and facing yet another day and night of not painting.

In the years when I was painting I sold enough to earn, not a steady living, but sometimes a relatively good one. Now I have to depend on the stupid antiques. The antiques were my mother's business. I was never interested in them. But now, since she's died, whenever I need money I take something out of that barn that's crammed full of her old junk and I phone through her contacts until I find someone to buy from me. I sell below what things are worth so someone is always out there willing to deal. But one day that barn will be empty, and then what will I do? I'll be faced not only with not painting, but not eating as well.

There's a lot that's my mother's fault. If she hadn't died, I wouldn't have to deal with all the crap she left behind. I wouldn't have to make my supper and wash my clothes. But she wasn't as good at housework after she had the stroke anyway. The worst of it, though, is that she decided to collect the early furniture from the local factory. It was a good choice in that it's easy to find—practically everyone has one of those old tables in the garage—and it's worth money, but no one in the area will buy any of it. There's too much locally. So this means I have to go miles out of town just to get rid of one bloody chair. Rare china patterns would have been a better choice, and much easier to store.

I suppose, if I think about it, there's a lot that is my father's fault. My mother is my father's fault. If he hadn't been depressed and unable to work, she would never have started the stupid antique collecting. If he hadn't killed himself, I would never have had to move back home to take care of my mother after she had the stroke. That would have been his responsibility.

My father was useless, really. He didn't even do his death very well. He hung himself in the woods behind the cabin. He'd moved into the cabin a year before, preferring to live there rather than in the house with my mother. I was well away by then, living in the city, working in a bar, and painting. I hadn't been home to see my parents all that year my father lived in the cabin. It was a shock to get that call. I was so used to my father's depressive inertia that it was a shock to hear he'd done something about it. But his death was a sad mistake, just like his life. He'd hung himself in the woods behind the cabin, taking one of the kitchen chairs to stand on; but he must have changed his mind after he kicked the chair away and was swinging in the noose. When they found his body his hands were up around his throat, trying to pry the rope away from his neck.

My father's depression found me after his death, and it

got so bad for a while that I had to go into hospital. The pills they put me on took away the desire to paint, and so I stopped that. It all happened so quickly. It was as though my father's miserable spirit flew out of him when he died and flew down to nest in me.

And so much is Alice's fault. I thought it was a good idea to offer her the cabin to live in when I found out she needed somewhere to stay. I was so lonely I knew the company would be good for me. And she was pretty and sad, a combination I've always liked. I lied about my mother still being alive in order to get her to trust me enough to risk living in the woods with a total stranger, but I thought that once she was out here we'd get along and things would work out. Things working out meant that we would fall in love and I would be happy and start painting again. Never mind that it has been so long since I've been in love that I've actually forgotten how it works and what it feels like. My sex life for years has consisted of jerking off to porn, and there are some days I can't even bring myself to do that. It feels too sad. There are some days I feel so pathetic that I can't even be bothered to undo my pants and pull my dick out.

It soon became clear to me, after a few days of Alice living in the cabin, that an affair with her was not going to happen. She was in love with Rachel, the woman who studies wolves. I heard them having sex. I'm ashamed to say that I crept around the cabin and spied on them. Well, I'm not really ashamed to say that. It's my property. I have a right to know what goes on here.

Actually I spied on them all the time. I could never see very much because the cabin was often in darkness, or lit only by an oil lamp. The light from an oil lamp holds close to the lamp, wraps around it. It's not a brave light, that's how I've always thought of it. But even if I couldn't see much, I could hear plenty. I've spilled a lot of my seed on the ground outside that cabin.

And even though Alice was in love with Rachel, she was still nice to me. I could go over in the evenings and we'd sit on the front steps of the cabin and talk. Just being able to talk to someone again was such a relief. I hated living with Mother at the end when I had to take care of her, but she was there to talk to. That's why I got the dog, for company after she'd gone. The few people who still kept up with me had suggested I move back to the city after Mother died, but I couldn't face sorting through and packing up all the junk in the farmhouse, so I got the dog instead. I don't throw anything away because I can always see a use for it, even if that use never materializes, and I have to say that this is often the case. There's a lot of stuff in the house. A lot of stuff in the house and a lot of stuff in my head. It was a relief to offload some of what was in my head in those evening conversations with Alice.

I talked to her about painting and she convinced me to try it again. Having someone to report back to made a difference, gave me a sort of deadline. When I was just here by myself I found it easy to remain in a state of procrastination. I would get easily distracted by anything. I would walk from room to room and pick up a magazine and start reading an article on something I wasn't even interested in, or pick up one of the military artifacts that I keep around the house because I have a bit of a thing for weapons, and I would think about its uses or its history. Distraction operated as forgetting and forgetting gave me a little peace.

The first time I set up the easel I got exhausted by the possibility of all that lay before me. I set up the easel and propped a canvas against it and then I had to go and lie down. What if I failed when I tried to paint again? What if I failed as much at painting as I was failing at not painting? By actually attempting it again I would know the truth, and if I did fail, then I would just be caught in a total web of failure. It is not pretty what goes on inside my head. No wonder I am always tired.

After I'd rested off the trauma of setting up the easel I brought the brushes and the box of oils out. It was shocking to see the tubes of paint squeezed in the middle where I'd once applied them to my palette in a fever of creativity. I felt like I was looking at an object in a museum, it all seemed that distant from me.

I had to rest after that too, of course. It was days later before I finally got around to painting, and even then I had to get drunk first and all my lines were shaky. But the next morning, after I awoke from where I'd passed out on the couch and I looked at what I'd done, there was one line that was good, one line that could stay. That was all the encouragement I needed to keep going. The next day when I looked at that line it was still good, and it was still good the day after that. I started and I couldn't stop. All those years of not painting suddenly became unblocked in an instant and all the silence poured out of me onto the canvases. I felt happier than I've ever felt. I didn't drink as much. I forgot to eat. I went off my meds. My thoughts didn't torture me the way they usually did and I began to realize that perhaps I suffered from an overactive imagination and that when it wasn't working for good it was working for evil. Being back at painting made me feel as close to being a normal person as I'd ever felt.

I painted a still life of rotting fruit. I painted what was outside the window of the farmhouse. At night I painted what I remembered being outside the window, and those paintings were often better than the ones where I worked from reality.

Loneliness closes one down. Loneliness is the lid tightening on the jar. It forces one to live airless. I had been shrinking my life down to one room, a handful of thoughts, the same tired, sad habits. When Alice came to live in the cabin, just the presence of someone else on the property was enough to spiral my life out again. By not controlling everything in my surroundings I felt less out of control.

Of course, it couldn't last.

Why do we know that when something is good it will not last, as surely as we know that when something is bad it will? One day I went to the easel and the painting I was working on seemed meaningless. I flipped through the other paintings I had stacked up against the wall and saw that they were also terrible. I had been doing them under some illusion and now I could see the truth. The truth was exactly as I feared. The paintings were awful. I was a failure.

I got very drunk then. I started drinking in the morning and I kept it up all day and through the evening. I sat in my armchair and drank and looked at the paintings until I couldn't bear to look at them any more. Then I went over to them and put them one at a time onto the easel and I painted them all over black.

Who was I to think that I could be who I wanted to be?

It was much later when I heard Alice's car in the driveway. I must have fallen off to sleep and the headlights shining through the front window of the farmhouse woke me up again. Alice. It was all her fault. I was much worse off now than I'd been before she got here. I stumbled out of the chair and went over to the window. I meant to open the window and yell out to her that everything was her fault, but when I got to the window I remembered that this window didn't open, and I could see, from the halo of the porch light, that Alice wasn't alone. Someone opened the passenger door of her car and stepped out. I thought it would be Rachel, but it wasn't. It was a boy. It was the boy who used to come and wait for his dog at the woods behind Cooper's farm with the rest of us. What was his name?

Jamie. He hung around Alice like a puppy. He didn't like that she paid so much attention to Rachel. He wanted all of Alice's attention for himself.

They walked on down the driveway in front of the car and I lost sight of them. I staggered back to my armchair and collapsed into it. A cloud of dust rose around me like fog. I felt like yelling at Alice, but I couldn't really do that if she had company. But why was the boy here? It was late. I squinted at my watch. It was almost midnight. What was she doing with the boy?

I thought of the times I'd crept around the cabin and spied on Alice and Rachel being lesbo sluts. Alice must have brought the boy home to have sex with her. Maybe she had brought him back to have sex with the both of them. Hot schoolboy sex. That must be it. I lurched up from the armchair again, full of indignation. He was so young. I would have to go over there and save him. Or at least watch.

Why did Alice want everyone except me?

I meant to take the bayonet, but I couldn't find it. I pretended I kept all the antique weapons in the house in case I was robbed, for protection, but really I liked playing with them. Instead of the bayonet the speargun seemed fine. I grabbed it and, using it for balance, set off down the path through the woods towards the cabin.

I had lost a lot of my momentum when I got to the cabin. I had tripped on a root on the path and fallen down hard, and my knee felt wobbly and bruised by the time I charged up the cabin steps. I had meant to burst in and surprise them, but I had trouble with the door, and by the time I'd fumbled it open and staggered into the cabin, I felt deflated of my purpose and wished I hadn't come.

Alice and Jamie were seated at the table. They looked genuinely alarmed to see me, but it wasn't because they were caught out. It was because I lurched rather threateningly into the cabin brandishing the old speargun.

Alice was kind to me, I'll say that for her. She was kind, even though the boy swore at me. I don't think that boy's ever liked me. But Alice was kind when I sat down on the bed and cried. She and the boy took me back along the path to the farmhouse. I felt exhausted from my journey to the cabin and sat meekly in my chair while Alice made me a cup of tea. The boy had wandered off to explore, which I was glad about. I hadn't asked Alice why he was here, but I couldn't be bothered to now. It was obviously nowhere near what I had thought and I wasn't really interested in other scenarios. I'd wanted to burst in on Alice and the boy having sex. I'd really wanted that.

"Here you are." Alice hands me a cup of tea and, moving a stack of newspapers out of the way, perches on the edge of the couch opposite. "Do you want me to call someone for you?"

"No." There's really no one to call, but I don't say that. I don't want to say that. It's too sad.

The tea tastes better than the whisky had earlier. "You can go if you want," I say. I don't want her feeling sorry for me. I feel sorry enough for myself. "I can manage from here."

"Well, I don't think you have been managing," says Alice. "That's just the point."

But she rises wearily from the couch, takes her tea mug into the kitchen, even though she could have just left it on the floor with the piles of other dishes that are there. I hear her move about, looking for the boy, and then they both come back into the living room. The boy has his hands behind his back, but I'm too tired to be bothered to find out what he's stolen from me.

"Go back to the cabin, Jamie," says Alice. "I'll be along soon."

The boy leaves. I hear the kitchen door close and the scuff of his shoes on the porch, and then all is quiet again.

I miss the dog. I miss the way he paid attention to what I was doing, but never judged me. I miss his woolly shape. I miss how alert he was, how he listened to noises and divided them into threats and nothing to worry about. He barked at threats. He went back to sleep when there was nothing to worry about.

Today has not been a good day. I have truly recognized my loneliness. That's what I have done today. The manic bout of painting and the drunken jaunt over to the cabin in the middle of the night were just attempts to break out from the slow tomb of my days. They were reckless, foolish, extreme gestures, but they were fuelled by desperation, and what is horrifying to accept is not the gestures, but the motivation. And the trouble is that crazy gestures like those only drive people away instead of bringing them in closer. When you are so lonely, you want to take a quick leap out, even though the only true way in or out of anything is by increments. I got here by degrees. I can only get out the same way. I know that, but I don't have the patience to last another minute here.

I need to say something nice to Alice to prove that I can be a good person.

"You're kind," I say, and she looks at me strangely.

It's no use, really. I try again and it's worse. She waits a polite amount of time and then she leaves.

The living room looks dusty and squalid. From outside I can hear an owl, and if I listen hard, there's the rough hum of cars out on the highway. This is my world. I can no longer imagine that it will ever be anything different. I have gone to the edge of it and back again.

I put down the mug of tea on the floor beside the chair, and I pick up the whisky bottle.

walter

I watched the story of Lily's death on television. For a week, every day, while the hunters gave testimony to the police, they had it as the lead story on the news. They showed the woods and the fields behind Cooper's farm. The first day they showed the corpse of one of the dogs, but there were complaints following this and so they didn't show it again. They showed the hunters, looking awkward and nervous in their suits, entering and leaving the police station.

They never showed the dead girl. I was glad of that.

I sat in my reclining chair in the basement of my daughter's house and I watched the evening news. Georgie lay on the elevated footstool between my feet when the chair was in its launch position. He liked to watch television. I tried to see if he had a reaction when they showed the woods or the body of the wolf dog, but he seemed as unconcerned as ever. Perhaps he'd forgotten that episode of his life already. Dogs are really just as good at forgetting as remembering if it suits them.

In their defence, the hunters talked about the number of dogs that had been in those woods and how fierce they'd been when confronted. It amazed me to think that my little Jack Russell had lived out there with those wild things, had been a part of that pack. I couldn't make the leap between the mangy corpse of the wolf dog and the small curl of fur and bone and blood that lay contentedly between my tartan slippers on the recliner.

"What happened out there?" I sometimes asked Georgie, but, of course, there was no way I was ever going to find out from him. But I did learn, from the hunters' testimonies, that the dogs had survived largely on a diet of rodents and rabbits, and if there was one thing I did know about Georgie—he was very good at hunting. I'm sure his skill at killing rodents would have made up for his small stature and established him a significant place in the pack.

My daughter calls where I live in her basement a "suite," but it's really only one big room and a bathroom. I eat upstairs with my daughter, her husband, and the baby, although some days I can't face that and tell them I've already eaten, and I hide out down here with cheese and crackers and a tumbler of Scotch. There are no windows in my basement suite and the floor is always cold because it's just cement under the thinnest membrane of carpet. Once I thought I'd put some underpad down beneath the carpet and I pulled up a section, but it was too much kneeling for my arthritic bones and so I gave up on that project. On the concrete under the piece of carpet I had pulled up I found a series of paw prints embedded into the cement. Raccoon prints. When the house had first been built and the basement had been poured, a raccoon must have wandered across the floor one night, through the empty, half-finished building. I can't imagine how many hours it would have taken that poor raccoon to get the cement off his paws.

I used to live in a two-storey house, and now I live in one big room. Sometimes this is hard to reconcile. After my wife died I whittled the contents of our home down into this basement. It was a horrible job, having to weigh each item on a scale of nostalgia and usefulness, having to decide, decide, decide, for days at a time. This goes. This can be sold. This I can never bear to part with.

I sold the house and paid off the mortgage and put the rest in the bank. I pay Amy and Doug rent for this room and they feed me and are my support in case anything goes wrong. I am often sick. I have a lot of ailments. I lie in bed at night and review them, working from the top down. My eyes have cataracts. I think I am developing arthritis in my neck. I have rotator cuff in my right shoulder. Often I have chest pains. Sometimes my digestion is troublesome. My hips hurt when it rains. My knees are bad. My ankles swell in the heat. I might have gout.

When my wife was alive she would at least feign interest in my health problems. But Amy has a baby to look after and she is less bothered with how I'm doing. I often think that having me in the basement is the same for her as having stuffed me into some closet. It's not that she is heartless. It's just that she is always busy.

The baby was never popular with me, or with Georgie. It makes too much noise, and always at the worst times. Georgie has snapped at it. He has snapped at it because the baby has snatched one of his toys, or is playing with something that looks like one of his toys. Dog toys and baby toys are remarkably similar.

The snapping was the reason Amy and Doug gave for getting rid of the dog. They felt justified in protecting their baby. Really, they should have just kept the little bugger away from Georgie's fluffy squirrel.

But now that the miracle of Georgie's return has occurred they have grudgingly agreed to let him stay, provided I don't let him anywhere near their precious baby. I have no intention of ever letting Georgie out of my sight again. Every time I go outside, or go for a drive in the car, I take the dog with me. The only place he doesn't accompany me is when I make a visit to the bathroom. These days I make a lot of visits to the bathroom. I wonder, am I developing prostate trouble.

Georgie came out of the woods because he had a piece of metal stuck in his paw and the pad had festered and grown infected around it. A quick trip to the vet's, some antibiotic cream, and a bandage that he chewed off the first night was all the treatment required. I often wonder about his decision to leave the woods. Did he realize that with a sore paw he wouldn't be able to hunt and he wouldn't be of any use to the pack? Or did he remember me and remember that whenever he had come to me with an injury before, I had made it better for him? Perhaps the other dogs suggested, in their telepathic dog way, that he leave the woods, that they'd no longer be able to feed him if he could no longer get food. I do know that it had been a decision, and given what happened to the other dogs, it had been a very good decision to come out of the woods when Georgie did.

What was more miraculous than Georgie's living in the woods with the dogs was the fact that Lily had lived there too. There was almost a full three-week period between the day she disappeared and the day she was shot. All that time she had been living as an animal. That's how they referred to it on the news—*living like an animal. She didn't seem human,* said the hunters. I wonder how Lily thought of it for herself. I know she was damaged and not the brightest person because of that, but it seems she never tried to leave the dogs and that must also have been a decision she made. And just as I want to know why Georgie left, I want to know why Lily stayed.

I suppose part of it must have been because she was able to be reunited with her dog. But why wouldn't she want to bring the dog with her out of the woods? Why wouldn't she want to take the dog home? Was she afraid it would be sent away again? I think this over and over, lying at night in the total black of the basement suite, after I have gone over my list of ailments. Did Lily's brain damage make her closer to an animal state than the rest of us? Would a so-called normal person have remained in the woods with the dogs?

"What did it feel like to be out there?" I ask Georgie, but he just grunts and burrows farther under the blankets.

I have been in the woods before. I have been camping. We used to go camping a lot when my daughter was young. But then, as always when I have been in the woods, I knew where the car was. I knew how to get back home again. I don't know what I'd feel like if I couldn't depend on those certainties. If I was in the woods without any guarantee of getting out, what would it be like? Would I have to depend on the essentials of who I am for my survival?

I lie in bed in the dark envelope of this room, listening to Georgie snore and the static whine of the upstairs TV, and I can't decide which traits of mine would be useful for survival.

I am stubborn. I am tenacious. I am well organized. I am loyal—but here I have to interrupt myself and be reminded that I haven't been very loyal to my daughter in the dislike I feel for her baby. I can be loyal, when I choose to be. I used to be strong before my body developed all these annoying tics and stutters.

Am I brave? I think so. I handled my wife's dying well, never letting myself slide into self-pity, always being respectful of her wishes. But did I love my wife as passionately as I had loved an earlier girlfriend, Claire? No. And if it had been Claire who was dying of cancer, wouldn't I have sobbed and carried on, thrown myself wholeheartedly into grief? I have always done the thing that I can bear. I haven't lived honestly. And that's what I think living in the woods with the pack of dogs would have been about. They would have had no choice but to live honestly.

At the end of the investigation they don't arrest anyone for the killing of Lily Steadman. There will be an inquest, but until then it's been ruled an accidental death. The hunters are absolved of guilt, although the one hunter who actually shot the girl looks no more comforted by the decision than he would be if the opposite were true. A few days after the investigation is over they find his body behind the old factory on the river. He has shot himself. Blown his brains out.

The last thing they say about the whole episode concerns

the pack of dogs. It seems that not all the dogs were killed by the hunters, and the ones that remain have again formed themselves into a pack. They've been spotted leaving the woods to make forays out to the neighbouring farms. They are still a problem, said the reporter on the newscast. There is a reluctance to hunt them after what happened to Lily, but I'm sure the memory of that will dim, and once again the dogs will be culled.

Thinking about the dogs and listening to the sad story of what happened to Lily have made me remember the people who used to gather at the edge of the woods out back of Cooper's farm, trying to call their dogs home. I liked being out there with those people. I liked feeling that we were bound together, that I belonged somewhere. I remember that Alice was particularly kind to me that day we all got lost in the woods behind Malcolm Dodd's farmhouse.

I decide to put Georgie into the car and drive over to Malcolm's place. I have it in my mind to go and see Alice again. I want to talk to her about what happened to Lily. I've been agonizing over the fact that we could have done a better job trying to find her. Why didn't we call the police? I can't remember now, although I think there was a reason at the time. Perhaps I am starting to develop Alzheimer's?

It's mid-afternoon when I drive up the rutted, bumpy driveway that leads to the farmhouse. I stop the car by the porch steps, afraid to drive any farther down the track as my muffler is already loose and I don't want it to fall off from all the jostling. I get out of the car. The air feels cooler here than it does in town. I wish I'd worn something other than a sweater.

The farmhouse door opens and Malcolm pokes his head out.

"Walter," he says. "What are you doing here?"

I come up the porch steps towards him. "Terrible about that girl, wasn't it?" I say. We stand facing each other.

Malcolm looks tired and he hasn't shaved in a few days. "I just thought I'd pop by and see how you and Alice were doing."

"Alice has gone," says Malcolm.

"Gone? Where to?"

"I don't know. She just left." Malcolm looks down at Georgie. "Too bad about the girl," he says. He opens the door. "Do you want to come in?"

I am disappointed that Alice isn't here. I was looking forward to seeing her much more than I was looking forward to seeing Malcolm, but I step into the farmhouse anyway. Georgie darts between Malcolm's legs and races away to explore the new territory.

"Did you hear," I say, "that the dog pack is now being led by your dog?"

"Sidney?"

"Hard to believe they're still considered a nuisance when they're being governed by an orange poodle."

"Poodles are very smart," says Malcolm defensively. "I did a lot of poodle research before I bought that dog."

We are silent. I have said the wrong thing, insulted Malcolm's absent dog, and I can feel he has grown all bristly towards me.

Georgie trots happily back to me with what looks like a pork chop in his mouth.

I look beyond where Malcolm and I are standing, to the sordid interior of the farmhouse. Everywhere there are piles of books and magazines, plates, and broken bits of furniture. "It's an awful mess in here," I say, before I can stop myself.

Malcolm looks behind him at the state of his living space. "Awful," he says, in agreement, and he rubs his forehead as though looking at the mess has just given him a terrible headache.

When I had to take apart the life my wife and I shared, I

was able to see how it was put together. We lived largely on an island of nostalgia. I suppose this is the natural territory of the elderly, but it shocked me to realize how much we operated our lives as a sort of museum, keeping the past on display in every room. It was easy to get rid of keepsakes. It was harder to dispense with the present. I spent ages agonizing over what to do with my wife's clothing, or deciding what kitchen things I should take with me to Amy's. I happily sold our ancestral furniture, and couldn't part with the notebook where we'd listed every type of bird that had ever used the winter bird feeder in our backyard.

I may not be brave, but I do know what is truly valuable. I may not have lived honestly, but I do know how to pack a box full of things that aren't necessary. I do know how to throw stuff out.

"You know what you need?" I say.

"What?" says Malcolm, looking startled.

Georgie is crunching the pork chop in the space between my feet.

"You need some organizing," I say.

And so this is how it ends up. Not what I would have imagined for myself, not what I would have foreseen from the beginning, but right nonetheless.

Georgie and I move into the farmhouse and I organize Malcolm Dodd. I clear out a lot of the junk. I spruce the place up. When I finish with the house I move on to the barn. Malcolm's mother had collected a fine number of valuable pieces of furniture from the early days of the factory, and after making an inventory of the stock, I decide to reopen her antiques business. Malcolm and I make an arrangement wherein I take a percentage of the profits, he takes a percentage, and we put a percentage back into the business. He helps with the dealing sometimes, although it's always better when he doesn't. He has a nervous sort of energy that distracts me and I feel relieved on the days when he decides to concentrate on his painting.

I don't think Malcolm Dodd is a very good painter, but what do I know about painting anyway? At night, when he is watching his pornography, I sometimes sneak into the room he uses as a studio and have a look at what's on the easel. It's usually a tangled web of lines and colours. If I look hard, I might be able to see a bowl of apples or a tree, but often the subject of the painting remains a mystery to me. I cannot really see the value in it, although I will often like a particular colour. There was a red in one of the paintings that was deep and yet shimmering, like the sun going down underwater. The red outlined what looked like a range of hills, and I did think about that red after I had left the studio. It did stay with me, not quite a feeling, not nearly a memory, but something lasting; so I suppose one could determine that painting a success—at least with me.

When I think about it, I think the red lasted for me as a taste lasts in your mouth after something you've just eaten. The taste is so much less than the food was, but it's also something other than a memory because it's the echo of something so recent. What is it then? It's not a memory, but rather it's a barrier against forgetting.

That's what I think of this life now, my life, when I lie awake at night in my room upstairs, Georgie snoring on the bed and the moon unnervingly bright through the window. Memory is a barricade against forgetting; light is a bulwark against darkness; life is a flex against the stillness of the grave. Maybe that's what I'm trying to do here, clear a space in all the debris, through all the anxieties and worries, where I can just exist, easily and simply, entire, for as long as I have left.

* * *

Amy and Doug did not mind when I left the basement suite of their house. I gave them some money from my savings to help them out. They are struggling with the new baby and the mortgage, with the realities of what they thought they wanted. I can see that, now that I no longer feel like their prisoner. I have even had them out here to the farmhouse, and even though they don't quite know what to make of Malcolm, they stayed longer than they said they were able to both times they came.

Malcolm and I have an odd but harmonious domestic arrangement. It is not ideal, but it is satisfactory. And it must be pleasing to him too because he drinks less now than he did when I first moved in. And now that there are those two living in the cabin with their dog, it often feels as if I have a family again, and I am unexpectedly grateful for this. It's not that Amy and Doug weren't my family, but here I get to do something, have some sort of role. Here I get to feel as though I belong to something bigger than myself.

The pack in the woods continues to grow. There's talk that the dogs have been joined by coyotes, that some of the dogs have mated with coyotes. The pack was seen running down a calf on a nearby farm and ripping it to pieces. And one night, on that same farm, the farmer was driving his tractor back through the fields in the dark and the whole pack of wild dogs ran alongside the tractor, growling and chewing at the tires.

In another city, hundreds of miles away from here, a pack of wild dogs made the news because it killed a woman jogging through the woods in the middle of the afternoon. The dogs brought her down and tore out her throat. Mercifully, she was found before they could begin the process of eating her body.

This story sends panic through our city again about the problem of our wild dogs. But the memory of Lily Steadman's killing is still too fresh and there is still a great deal of opposition to slaughtering the dogs.

It won't always be the same, though. I know that the day will come when the pack will grow too large and troublesome, and once again hunters will go into the woods to gun the dogs down.

It is almost winter now. There is frost on the window this morning. I sit up in bed. Georgie stretches his corpulent doggy self and gives a satisfied groan. He is getting fat off all the table scraps here. His skin is as tight as a sausage.

"How do you think they're doing out there?" I ask him, but he remains asleep.

He sleeps a lot now, what with the extra weight he's put on and winter arching its back against the windows. I can't help thinking that he'd be in much better shape if he were still living in the woods with the dog pack. Here he seems soporific with the lack of challenge in this life. His days are easy now, and not filled with danger, but what does he have to measure himself against?

Perhaps I never could have lived honestly. Perhaps I would have faltered before my desires if I'd been brave enough to admit them and brave enough to fight for them. Perhaps it is better to live long and lazy than short and intense. Perhaps my understanding of life would be no greater if I'd lived more honestly.

There is a cardinal on the tree outside my window. The flash of red is bright, like arterial blood, like the slash of red I remember from Malcolm's painting.

Perhaps this recognition, this taste of remembered life, is all I get on this earth.

Perhaps it will be enough.

rachel

I couldn't find the wolves. That was the start of it. Even though we'd heard them the night before so close by, when I went into the forest after them, I could find no trace of the pack.

I tromped through the forest, getting bloody with bug bites and more and more frustrated at the apparent futility of my quest. I followed animal trails through the trees. I went to the places where I'd seen the wolves before. All to no purpose. And in the end, when I was hungry and sweaty and exhausted by my efforts to find the wolves, it was hard not to blame Alice.

I had lost myself. It was that simple. I had allowed myself to become subsumed in someone else, and it felt terrible. I had lost the ability to track the wolves, to be attuned to their presence, because I had transferred that affinity over to Alice. My close link to the wolves defined for myself who I was, and without that, who was I? Being connected to another human being was much less secure than understanding the wolves. I didn't want that lack of control. Not at all.

I sat on a tree stump, miserable in the buzzing, piney air, with the flies circling my head and the sweat trickling down the back of my neck, and I realized it couldn't go on. My relationship with Alice.

Out in the forest, lost to the wolves and myself, I sat on the tree stump and I began to make my list of reasons why it could never work with Alice. I began to compile my excuses to use against her.

When I left to go into the forest, I was a dog, and when I returned to the camp that evening, I was a wolf again.

* * *

Love itself was growing burdensome. I felt obligated by it and I knew that eventually I would treat it badly, or be betrayed by it. It is always better to leave someone before they can leave you.

Alice and I had suffered similar damage from our earlier lives. I knew that, and I thought that the loneliness we solved by being together would make us free. But instead it bound us together in a way that soon felt suffocating.

Now I live out in the woods again and I feel cleansed by the solitude. There is no one to answer to, no one to disappoint. I spend my days observing the wolf pack and my nights sitting in the cabin writing up my notes. Once a week I go into town for supplies and to collect my mail. Once a month I have dinner with the three other biologists in the study who are observing the other wolf packs. This is the life I had before I met Alice, and I am happy to return to it. The days I spend out here are good days. They go mostly as I want them to.

The wolves have become used to my presence. They seem to know I mean them no harm, and as long as I keep my distance, they tolerate me. I never try to get nearer to them than I should. I know that being tolerated is the most one can hope for from a wild thing.

I still think about what happened to Lopez, and I feel bad that I allowed the possibility of that. I made a mistake in thinking I could keep a wolf pup as a pet. I should have just let him die instead of taking him into the human world and having him suffer so much at the end. I thought I could prevent him from being shot, and yet he was shot all the same.

I think too about Lily Steadman. I remember how we stood in the field behind Cooper's farm and we watched the hunters come out of the woods with the body of the girl and the bodies of the dogs. Alice and I had gone into the woods to try to find Lily once, but we hadn't been able to locate her. Now I think it was because we couldn't respond to anything outside the vortex of our attraction to each other when we were together. All we ever found was ourselves, whatever else we were looking for. But then I thought that perhaps we'd been wrong in thinking that the girl had had the notion to go into the woods after the dogs.

The three of us stood there by the truck, watching the grim procession make its way across the field. I hadn't wanted the boy to come, but Alice wouldn't leave him, and now he stood there as his dead dog was carried past him. It was wrong for him to have to see that. He will remember it forever and that betrayal will never soften. It will never make enough sense for him to be able to forgive it. I was angry at Alice for insisting that he come with us. And I was angry at myself for not getting us there in time to have been able to stop what happened to Lily and to the lovely wild dogs.

I have been betrayed so many times that, of course, it is what I know and what I will eventually do myself. Never trust anyone who has been betrayed. Betrayal never loses its edge, never really goes away.

That moment in the field was really the last time Alice and I were together. I never stopped loving her, that's the truth; but on the drive back to the cabin I could feel that her love for me had made her vulnerable and needy, and I despised that in her. I thought she should have been stronger than that. She should have been stronger than loving me had made her. She had collapsed her life into mine with a certainty I found claustrophobic. I couldn't wait to drop her and the boy back at the cabin, and I drove off feeling nothing but relief to be rid of the both of them.

I followed the inquest in the papers. I felt sorry for the hunter who had shot Lily and I wasn't surprised when he took his own life. I wish Lily hadn't been killed, mostly, of course, because she didn't deserve to be, but partly because

I would have liked to have known what it was like to live with the wild dogs as she did. I keep my distance from the wolves, but there is also the desire to be able to do what Lily did and live in the midst of what is wild.

I don't let myself think this often, but I sometimes wonder if what I felt most trapped by—love—was, paradoxically, the wilderness I could have entered. Maybe to be truly wild is to trust completely. What would have happened if I had really trusted Alice? What would have happened if I had come out from the trees down to the glow of that fire?

But I think this only late at night, when I wake to doubt and darkness, to the fast flutter of my own heart and the rustle of night at the windows of the cabin. In the wide span of day I am convinced anew of the rightness of my decision to leave Alice.

And I think of this—how I drove back last week from town through the early November darkness, and as I rounded a bend in the deserted country road, I came upon a fox that had just been hit by a car. It was clearly dead, a halo of dark blood around his head and the body twisted unnaturally, as though it were a wrung-out red towel. I slowed the car because there was another shape beside the first one, and when I got closer I could see that it was another fox, unhurt, sitting by the body of the dead fox. Its eyes in my headlights were flat and unafraid. It must have been the mate of the first fox. They must have been crossing the road together and now this fox didn't quite know what to do except to keep this uneasy vigil over the body of its mate. It didn't move on as I drove past, and I knew that if it stayed sitting there for long, it would be hit by the next car that came fast around the bend in the road.

This is what love makes possible. This is how it can end up and this is why it is to be feared. I never want to be that fox. I never want to feel that pain. And I am not talking about the dead fox, but the living one.

I don't believe love is good for everyone. Autonomy is a greater enabler. I'm sure of that. I don't have to look further than the wolves. The tensions and stresses in the wolf pack are enormous—all the testing of status and affection, all the jockeying for position within those twin hierarchies. The situation of the lone wolf is much preferable. Most lone wolves have been driven out of a pack and they remain alone until they can find a new pack to accept them. Wolves being social animals, the lone wolf is not especially glad to be alone, but there is a serenity to its solitude that I have noticed and admired. It doesn't seem nearly as anxious or restless as the wolves that remain part of the pack.

What would love solve for me that I could not solve for myself?

But I do remember things, that's the problem. Even when I don't want to think about Alice and this past summer, incidents come swimming back to me. Sometimes I dream of her and hear her voice talking to me, saying something reassuring, and I wake in a panic, fearing she is in the cabin with me now, when I open my eyes to the mousy dark. She was so sad when I drove away from her, and yet when she appears in my dreams, she is always the one calming me.

Sometimes too I will come back to the cabin in the dark at the end of these brief fall days, and I will remember the feeling I used to have when I walked up to the doorway of the cabin where Alice lived on Malcolm's property. I can feel exactly, again, that potent mix of nerves and anticipation that filled me up entirely as I walked those few grassy steps between the truck and the rotted wooden steps of the cabin. It was a feeling of being completely where I was, and of moving forward into where I wanted to be. Now, when I enter this cabin at night I know just what to expect, and my head is filled with the list of tasks I hope to accomplish before going to bed.

Yesterday I walked home through the field that lies to the south of the cabin. It wasn't quite dark and the air was cold. It snowed a few days ago, and even though that thin layer of snow has melted, the air promises more to come. I walked through the field and the sun was going down along the edge, a rim of red encircling the grasses and the junipers. The whole field was covered in milkweed pods, all split open and drooping with silk and seed. I reached out my hand as I walked through the field, and I touched the soft silk of the milkweed, and I found that it was warm, much warmer than the outside air. I stopped and pulled the edges of the pods apart and put my hand inside against the silk of the plant and again, each time, it held heat. Each milkweed I reached into was the same. It couldn't be the heat of the day because there had been no sun to warm this field. Could the plant somehow make its own heat? Was each milkweed a kind of miniature furnace? I stood in the middle of the field and I thought about this, and suddenly I remembered the summer smell of milkweed and how I had walked down the driveway towards the cabin, towards Alice, and the scent of milkweed was heavy as a fog around me. And here, now, the pods are still warm from that day, like torches that have been lit and extinguished, studding the field of this November afternoon. It is as though what was once on fire can never really go out. There will always be enough heat left to show me how fiercely love once burned.

It started with the wolves but it ended with Lily Steadman being borne across the field by the hunters. I had hoped for so many things and not realized it. I had hoped that the dogs would stay free, that they would thrive in the woods. I had hoped that Lily really had gone in after them and that no one would be able to find her, and that she would live out her life, happy and wild. These were foolish, childish hopes. I knew that when I saw the hunters coming out of the woods with the bodies of the dogs and the body of Lily Steadman. They were unrealistic hopes, but they were activated by the lovely, wild gesture of the dogs going into the woods and Lily going in after them. These gestures were based on a trust I didn't possess and didn't know I really wanted until I saw the hunters walking towards us across the field behind Cooper's farm.

What I wanted, of course, was to be able to trust in love.

The boy was betrayed, and I was betrayed, and later Alice would be betrayed by me. We stood there and the hunters wove through the field grass towards us. The men looked solemn and afraid, and yet they carried the dogs and the girl with such, well, tenderness that it was hard to believe at first that what they carried in their arms was dead.

In that moment I couldn't reach out to Alice or Jamie to comfort them. I couldn't even bear to know what they were feeling, although I assumed it was similar to what I was feeling. The shock of what had happened and the sad inevitability of it had sunk me deep inside myself. I went down with it, and when I surfaced again, I had drifted away from the others.

Lily wouldn't have known what hit her. That's what they said in the press, at the inquest. The shot killed her instantly and she wouldn't have had time to register what was happening to her. I don't agree with that. I have seen animals shot, and I have seen people who have been blind-sided by grief. We always know what has hit us. We don't always know that it will kill us.

*   *   *

Have I really helped the wolves I study? I have trapped them and tranquilized them and fitted them with radio collars. I have used a helicopter to follow a pack across a frozen lake. What have I learned from all this? Migratory habits. Feeding habits. A little bit about the nature of a particular pack. What I have learned the most is how easily and frequently wolves are killed by humans.

A wolf can live up to thirteen years in the wild, but most wolves die before they are five years old. Some wolves die from starvation or accidentally fall through thin lake ice, but most of the wolves that die are shot, poisoned, or caught in wire snares that tighten around their throats, severing flesh and skin with each movement they make trying to escape from the noose of wire.

Radio-collared wolves are shot just as frequently as the wolves without collars. Sometimes the collar is mailed back to us by the hunter, but often it isn't. The collar is no protection for the wolf and I had hoped that it would be. Sometimes I get the death signal from one of the collars as the wolf is being killed, the heartbeat coming in fast and frantic over my headphones.

What good is a wolf? people will say when I confront them about having killed one.

What good are we?

People have always been afraid of wolves. Once the wolf was thought to be the devil in disguise. They have been villainized in fairy tales and folklore. But what is this fear, really? Is it not that we are afraid of what is wild within ourselves? Isn't the whole structure of society about trying to fit ourselves into smaller and smaller cages? The more confined we are by duty and love, the more our wilderness will be tamed and the more secure we expect to feel. But, of course, that's not true. We don't feel safe at all.

*   *   *

What do we mostly see when we see a wild animal? We see it running away from us. The truth of our communion with nature is the bird lifting from the branch, the white of the deer's tail as it bounds away into the undergrowth. We make a story up to connect all these fugitive glimpses together. The story might not be true at all, but the moments are, and somehow we find it unbearable to live with just the moment. Maybe we are afraid that life itself is as swift and unknowable as the wolf flickering behind the bars of the trees. And what I always think when I see the wolf moving fast away from me is this—if it would only slow down a little so I could get a better look, a longer look, then I might be able to learn something about it. I might be able to understand it.

Yesterday morning the strangest thing happened to me. I was up early, getting ready to leave for my day with the wolves. The pack has a den a few miles from this cabin. It is over an hour's walk, and I was preparing my lunch and loading up my bag with the radio receiver, with binoculars and a camera, extra gloves, and a flashlight in case I had to travel back in darkness. Before I head off each day I step outside to determine the temperature and I did that this morning, stepping out onto the small wooden porch in my socks. The air felt colder than the day before, and the low-slung grey sky looked to be harbouring a serious snowfall. I stood there, feeling the cold creep slowly through the wool socks into my toes, and I noticed a bird perched on the porch railing opposite me. It was a woodthrush, a bird that should have long since flown south to winter in Mexico.

"Hello there," I said, and the bird cocked its head at me, and then very deliberately hopped from the railing onto my hand. It perched there, gripping my finger with its small scaly feet, looking at me with its head tipped first on one side and then on the other. I could feel its grip tighten with even the smallest movement of my hand.

I don't have an answer for that. I don't know why the bird trusted me, or why Alice did, although I do believe that both these things did happen.

I stood on the porch of the cabin with the woodthrush clipped to my finger. My feet were growing thick with cold, but I wasn't going to be the first one who moved. Eventually the bird did fly off and I went back inside the cabin and gathered up the radio antenna and my bag and set off, purposefully, into my world. But I looked for that woodthrush all that day, and even though I haven't seen it again, I keep hoping it will come back. I can't pretend I don't want that to happen.

three

alice

I find the boy out by the road. He's walking and crying. I can see him swatting at his eyes with his hands, trying to wipe the tears away. I drive up alongside him, roll down the passenger window.

"Get in," I say, and he does.

He looks at me, all fierce and sad. "Why can't you take me with you?" he says, for he knows, as I know it, that I will be leaving this place.

I reach over and hold his face in both my hands, as I sometimes used to do with the dog when she was bad, and with you when you were good. "If it were possible," I say, "I would." Jamie has been the truest thing in my recent life. His heart has never faltered once towards me.

I pull onto the road. "Tell me where you live," I say, and we begin the sad process of taking him home.

When we pull into the driveway Jamie has stopped crying. He looks angry now, juts his jaw out, and rips the seat belt away from his body.

"You don't need to come in," he says.

"Yes, I do."

"Don't," he says, and he flings open the car door, slams it shut.

I follow him up the driveway to the front door of his house.

"I usually go in the back," he says, but I reach up and ring the bell.

When his mother sees him she hugs him hard to her, even though he struggles to get away. "Where were you?" she says, but Jamie just extricates himself from her embrace and looks embarrassed.

"This is Alice," he says, as though that's all the explanation he needs. "Is he home yet?"

"No," says his mother. "Hello," she says to me. I can see her puzzled look. She's trying to figure out if I'm some kind of authority figure, if Jamie's in trouble.

"I'm a friend of your son's," I say, but she looks even more confused by this.

"They shot Scout," says Jamie to his mother. "Killed him. And they killed Lily." He's started to untuck his shirt, lifts it up and over his head.

When I touched Jamie's back yesterday morning in the truck I had felt the ridges, rising like thick pieces of cord from his skin. I knew what they were because I have some of those myself. I knew what I'd see when he took his shirt off, and I was exactly right. The skin on his back was criss-crossed with welts.

"What are you doing?" asks his mother, looking from her son to me and back again. "Why have you taken your shirt off?"

"I'm just getting ready," says Jamie. "I'm just preparing myself. I'm making it easy for him." He says this with such anger that I can feel anger rise up in me. I can remember feeling exactly as he's feeling now.

I look right at Jamie's mother, into the green eyes that are the same as his. "I'm leaving this place," I say. "And if I had any rights to your son, I would take him with me. He deserves better than to be beaten."

Jamie turns and looks at me, and it's as if we all know the same thing at the same time, and knowing it makes us stronger than we thought we were a minute ago.

"You should go too," I say to his mother.

"Where would we go?"

"I think I know somewhere you could go," I say.

Jamie and his mother move into the cabin on Malcolm Dodd's property. And even though they're afraid Jamie's stepfather will show up there, the one time he does come he is confronted by Malcolm brandishing the speargun and he doesn't return again.

There is no choice for me but to leave this town. I felt that the day you left. And the thing is, I probably should have gone years ago. I stayed too long with not enough. Isn't that always the way?

I'll go and visit friends for a while, drive from city to city, see what opportunities there are for work and settling somewhere. And of course I'll want to drive up to where you are. But I won't do that.

At first I was so upset when you went that I couldn't do anything, couldn't think of anything else. Then I was angry, because I was worth more than the way that you left me.

But what remains now is the uncomplicated feeling of missing you. I miss talking with you. I miss being with you. I miss your particular take on the world and its creatures. I miss the happiness I felt simply being near you. I miss the person I was with you.

For ages after you had gone I looked for signs you might be coming back to me. A pileated woodpecker tapping his code of hunger into the trunk of a dead tree. Two hawks that drifted overhead. A fox running across a field. It seemed these unexpected glimpses of the natural world were a kind of hope. The flicker of recognized movement in the forest or the sky was a small rush of optimism. It meant something.

But then I thought that perhaps it wasn't the animal that was the true symbol, but the environment. Maybe I was fooled by the movement and couldn't see the landscape it occupied. The woodpecker and the hawks and the fox aren't the only things there. The message might just as well have been the hollow, desiccated tree, the empty sky, the hard, frozen field.

*   *   *

On the day I am leaving I wait by the end of the driveway for the school bus to drop Jamie off. He knows I'll be there. We have planned to spend these last hours together before I leave. I watch the bus doors open and slap back on their hinges. Jamie runs across the road without looking for traffic. He gets into the car and heaves his knapsack into the back seat. I look at him and he looks at me. I will miss this boy more than I will miss anyone or anything in this town.

"What shall we do?" I say, because it is his choice how we spend this last afternoon together.

"Let's go and wait for the dogs," he says.

So we drive to the edge of the fields behind Cooper's farm and I park the car where we parked the truck weeks ago. We get out and start to walk across the field. When we get to the edge of the trees, we stop. It seems a long time ago now when we all first gathered here.

"Are we calling?" asks Jamie. "Because I can't call for Scout any more. I can't call for him if he's dead."

"Can't you?" I say. Jamie still wants the dog to come back. That hasn't changed.

I stand in the place I always stood, and I yell Hawk's name into the trees, and I think of how you used to stand beside me here.

"Scout, Scout, Scout," yells Jamie, racing back and forth in front of me, exactly as he used to, bouncing the words off the trunks of the trees.

The wind pulls the branches and they move in green calligraphy against the darkening sky.

"Hawk," I yell, and just at the moment I shout the word, Hawk herself trots out from the trees. She's skinny and her coat looks all raggedy, but it's definitely my dog. She walks slowly up to me, casually, as though we've just been out for a walk and she's wandered ahead and I've had to call her back.

"Shit," says Jamie. He's stopped running, comes over to me.

"Hawk," I say again, and I drop to my knees and grab her by the thick fur on either side of her shoulders. I bury my hands in her fur and I lean over and touch my forehead to hers, and she stands there placidly, as she always does when I do this. I can feel the bones of her shoulders under my fingers and I can smell the rank scent of her breath.

"Alice," says Jamie. "Look." I open my eyes and look over Hawk's head and see a black dog standing just behind her. One of the black dog's ears is half gone and scabbed over.

"Who's that?" I say.

Jamie looks carefully at the black dog. "Dog?" he says tentatively, and the black dog wags her tail and whines. "It's Lily's dog," he says to me. "Wouldn't she like that?"

Jamie takes Dog back to live with him and his mother at the cabin and I take Hawk away with me.

The dog sits up in the front seat of the car, just as she used to, watching the scenery. We drive past the factory, the windows boarded over now, and a ribbon of police tape looping around the back, where that hunter shot himself.

I stop the car by the river, at the place where the water shoots down the waterfall, and I get out. The smell is sulphur and cold. The smell is winter coming on. The noise is what I sometimes hear in my head when I close my eyes at night—that thundering rush, all urgency and movement, as though the river is too slow for itself.

Hawk gets out with me at the river, and we stand there by the car. The water shooting by in front of us is brown from churning so fast along the riverbed.

I look back at the factory, hunkered down on the banks of the river. I remember my father coming out of that factory at quitting time, and I think how strange it is that in all the years I've been living in this town, I've never once seen the factory from the inside.

The dog pushes her nose into the palm of my hand, her old signal for wanting to get moving.

"Come on, then," I say, and we walk down towards the factory.

It is easy to pry one of the boards off a window and crawl in. I make Hawk stay outside the building because I'm afraid she'll cut herself on the broken window glass, and for a moment, when I crawl over the sill, I'm afraid she won't be there again when I come back out. But she is sitting on the ground by the window, looking up at me in an anxious sort of way, and I just have to trust that she won't disappear.

I can't go very far into the factory because there's only the light from the window I've entered to see by, that and a few streaks of daylight overhead through gaps in the roof.

The interior smells stale, smells of old wood and decaying animals. There are pigeon feathers on the floor, and rusted bits of metal. I can hear the river and I realize that probably, with the noise of the machines, the men who worked in this factory would never have been able to hear the river.

And as my eyes get accustomed to the dimness of the huge room, I can see how the wooden floor is warped from years of weight in the same place. There are large areas of sway where the machines sat. There are small hollows where the men once stood in front of the machines. Each man reduced to a dent the size of his feet.

Everything is movement or its monument.

When I get back outside the dog is still there. She walks back with me to the car, sits up straight in the front seat. When we get to the highway she drops down, curls into a ball, and goes to sleep.

Your leaving will not be solved by your coming back. But one does not preclude the other. And maybe that is always what there is to fear, in everything that happens—what we choose to love will choose to forsake us.

The truth is, I want you to come back. I don't think we're finished. I don't believe that all we were meant to have was something as brief as the red twist of the fox moving fast across the empty field.

I don't think any more that my life is about what has happened to me. It's about what I choose to believe. It's not what I can see, but what I think is out there.

And in the end, this end, here is what I believe.

The heart is a wild and fugitive creature.

The heart is a dog who comes home.

Acknowledgements

I would like to thank my agent, Frances Hanna, and my editors, Phyllis Bruce and Amy Cherry, for their wisdom and encouragement.

The lines from William Faulkner used as an epigraph are reprinted by permission of The Library of America.

I used a myriad of sources for the animal lore referenced in this novel, but I am particularly indebted to the following books: *Wolf Country: Eleven Years Tracking the Algonquin Wolves* by John Theberge and Mary Theberge, *Of Wolves and Men* by Barry H. Lopez, and *Way of the Wolf* by L. David Mech.

I would like to thank the pack I ran with during the writing of this book, for their kindness, patience, and care: Mary Louise Adams, Kelley Aitken, Susan Belyea, Elizabeth Christie, Craig Dale, Elizabeth Greene, Anne Hardcastle, Cathy Humphreys, Paul Kelley, Paula Leger, Susan Lord, Sharon MacKenzie, Barb Mainguy, Bruce Martin, Daintry Norman, Karen Pegley, Glenn Stairs, and Nathalie Stephens.

Thanks to Diane Schoemperlen for keeping the faith and to Joanne Page for those long walks over the ice.

Thanks to Emma Brooks and Kate Brooks for being wild puppies.

Sue Goyette, I couldn't have done this (or anything else) without you.

This book is for you, Jennifer Ross.